Box-Shaped Heart

Thomas Gahr

Printed in the United States of America

First Printing: 2013

20 Prospect Press ISBN 13: 978-0615807232

ISBN 10: 0615807232

www.boxshapedheart.com

Cover photo: A Winter Morning (1900-1910) Detroit Publishing Company Photograph Collection – Library of Congress LC-D4-34785

DEDICATION

To Karen, Alyssa, and Nathan for their constant support
and encouragement

ACKNOWLEDGMENTS

This novel would not have been possible without the help of others. My editor Meghan Pinson was a constant help in guiding a rookie through the process of writing a book, and being a cheerleader to keep me motivated despite my struggles with the rules of grammar and punctuation. I am also indebted to the work of Genesee County historian Ruth M. McEvoy whose definitive history on the City of Batavia made it possible to walk the streets of 1882 Batavia. Finally, I owe gratitude the late Don Carmichael whose illustrations of old Batavia lined the walls of the Richmond Memorial Library and stimulated the imagination of a shy little boy on summer afternoons long ago.

CHAPTER ONE

Batavia, N.Y., 1882

The noonday sun glinted off the steel rails and shimmered on the horizon until the train tracks disappeared in glimmering pool. The smokestacks of the Wiard Plow factory spewed out lazy black plumes into the cloudless sky. The station was quiet, save for a few wagons waiting to meet the train, and Newt Rowell waited on the platform as Irish laborers loaded crates into boxcars. Passengers sat in the shade of the platform fanning themselves. There was no sound but the buzzing of flies around the swishing tails of the horses. Taking his watch out of his vest pocket, Rowell checked the time. The train was late, but having waited this long to see his family, a few more minutes hardly seemed to matter. In the distance the bells of St. Joseph's rang out the Angelus.

He wondered if the Irishmen would stop their work to pray, but they kept to their task, which surprised him.

Newt had only seen his wife and daughters twice in the past six months as he and his partner, Palmer, got the box factory running in Batavia. The transfer of equipment from Utica had gone smoothly, production was picking up, and inventory had gone quicker than their calculations. He was glad of it. He had been working long hours keeping the books while Palmer tended to the shop floor.

Newt put his watch back into his pocket and removed a handkerchief. He lifted his hat and wiped the sweat from his brow. Just a few finishing touches and the house would be complete. It was larger and more spacious than the one they had rented in Utica. Newt had been renting an upstairs room in the Masse Building until now, but this time the girls would be staying in Batavia for good. Just that morning he'd placed a large vase of lilies in the front parlor, hoping Jennie would be pleased. This was a chance for them both to have a fresh start, away from the scandals, away from the worries, away from temptation.

Across the tracks on Jackson Street, people hurried between the storefront awnings to escape the sun. The population of the village was already over six thousand souls and seemed to grow by the day as immigrants arrived to fill the tenements on the South Side. Labor in Batavia was cheaper than in the Mohawk Valley, and land was plentiful. The move might prove more profitable than he had hoped.

Newt looked up and saw the train emerge from

the mirage, slowing as it crossed the switchyard near the factories and approached the station. The people on the platform stirred to life. Reaching into his coat pocket, he pulled out the paper bag of peppermint sticks that he bought on the way to the station. They were sticky and soft from the heat, but the girls would be thrilled to have them. Their absence from his life had made his heart ache. For months he'd had nothing but work and the fellowship of Palmer and the others in the Eagle tavern. How good it would be to have the girls' vivacious company filling the new house with laughter. How good it would feel to hold Jennie again.

The black iron beast steamed from every opening. Newt felt the heat of the engine on his face as it rolled past the platform. He scanned the windows of the coaches as they passed, looking for their faces. The conductor stepped down onto the platform as the train came to a stop in a long sigh of steam.

As Newt searched the crowd of passengers stepping off of the train, he heard the girls scream "Daddy!" Turning, he saw them running towards him across the platform.

He knelt down and caught them in his arms. "Oh, Daddy!" Clara said. "We missed you so much. We didn't think we would ever get here."

"You'll have to tell me all about the journey," Newt said, holding out the candy. "Look here, I brought you something."

The girls squealed as Newt turned his gaze toward the train to see Jennie step from the coach onto the platform, her long blonde hair tucked up under a wide-brimmed white hat. Even in this infernal heat, she seemed a center of calm, untouched and unfazed by the commotion around her. She smoothed the folds of her dress and looked down the platform at Newt and the girls huddled together in the crowd. Despite all that had happened, and all the troubles that had come before, he'd never felt more in love with her. Meeting his gaze, she smiled and looked upward and to the side in that way of hers that said "You are the silliest thing I have ever seen."

He stood and crossed the platform with a girl holding each hand. Jennie turned her head to offer her cheek for a kiss and reached up to steady her hat.

"I was beginning to worry the train would be late," Newt said, taking off his hat as he kissed Jennie.

"Tell me, Mr. Rowell, is it always this hellishly warm in Batavia, or is this something you have prepared special for us?" she said with a smile.

Newt grinned and took her by the arm, leading her to a hackney carriage. He lifted the girls into the hack and the driver took Jennie's hand to help her up the step. Newt arranged delivery of the luggage as Jennie fanned herself against the heat.

Returning, Newt instructed the driver, "One Twenty-three Bank Street, please."

"Is this a big city, Daddy?" Mary asked between licks of peppermint.

"Not as big as Utica, dear," Jennie said as the driver gave the reins a shake.

"But it's growing every day," Newt replied, looking at Jennie.

The carriage bumped over the rails and turned up

Jackson Street. The horse stirred the dust of the street as the train sounded its whistle to leave.

"It's been a dry spring," Newt said, "and this weather is unusual for May. The workshop has been an inferno this week."

Jennie looked at the wagons and horses moving down the street, then said, "It's not quite as bustling as Rochester. Newt, it was positively wonderful there. I wish we could have stayed for a bit."

"Perhaps we can get there some weekend once we've settled in," Newt responded.

The carriage turned out into Main Street past brick storefronts whose windows watched them through half-open sashes. The awnings above the doorways cast sharp shadows across the sidewalks. The women moved languidly between the stores in the heat, their bustles swaying behind them like horse tails. A man in a bowler standing in front of Hewitts' dry goods store nodded at Newt as they passed.

"How are the shops?" Jennie asked.

"The millinery seems nice, and the dry goods stores don't want for anything. I think you'll find everything you need here. There are advantages to being on the main railway line," Newt answered.

Jennie looked into the shop windows as they passed. "Yes, fortunately it should only take forty-five minutes to get to Rochester."

The business district stretched for six blocks between the white limestone courthouse and the pointed steeple of the Methodist church. Two- and three-story brick buildings stood shoulder to shoulder, set back from the dusty street by wide granite sidewalks. Farther down East Main Street the stone spires of more churches rose above the elm trees and the regal mansions of Batavia's rich. The hackney turned and headed north on Bank Street past shade trees as the commercial district gave way to wood-framed houses.

"Is our house far away?" Edna asked.

"No, dear, it is only a little ways up this street."

"What color is it?" asked Clara.

"Now, you don't want to spoil the surprise, do you?" corrected Jennie as they passed beneath a spring-green canopy of maple trees.

"Well, why don't you just see for yourself? It's right there," Newt said, pointing.

The carriage drew up in front of a dark red two-story house whose wide porch was set back just a few long strides from the street. Cream-colored gingerbread trim lined the gables of the roof and windows like lacework.

"Well, what do you think?" Newt asked as he stepped down onto the carriage block and turned to help Jennie.

"Oh, Newt, it seems hard to believe it's ours," she replied, narrowing her eyes as she surveyed the house.

"Yes, it does. It cost me dearly, but if business continues to go as well as it has, we shall make it up soon enough."

"I must say, I like the color. I was a little worried it would look like a firehouse when you wrote," Jennie said.

The girls jumped down from the carriage into Newt's arms and giggled as they ran across the yard and up the front steps. The fresh wood of the porch steps had yet to be painted, and little piles of sawdust still dotted the dirt.

"I haven't had a chance yet to see to the yard," Newt apologized, "but Mr. Reed next door has recommended a good gardener."

"You'll have to tell me about the neighbors," Jennie said as she stepped lightly across the hard-packed dirt, lifting the hem of her skirt. "I'd like to know more about them before we meet."

"In due time. First, you must have a look around your new castle."

The girls were already calling out to their parents as they stepped through the doorway into the whitewashed front hall. The mahogany banister glistened deeply with a fresh coat of varnish. To the side of the stairs a hallway ran back towards the kitchen. An archway on the left opened into the front parlor.

"Well, dear, I've left the inside for you to decorate as you wish. I am sure you'll take pleasure in applying your feminine touch." Newt held out his arm and led her into the parlor. The girls came scurrying back down the front steps and ran in behind them.

"Mother, this house has stairways in the front and the back!"

Seeing the vase of flowers on the table, Jennie stepped through the sliding pocket doors into the back parlor, as the smell of lilies filled the air. Sunlight streamed through the windows in the south wall, leaving rectangles of gold on the oak floor. She smiled as she said, "Well, Mr. Rowell, you certainly have seen to the details. They are lovely."

"I knew they were your favorite, dear."

"Would you like to see your bedroom now?" Newt asked the girls, leading them back into the hallway. The girls scrambled up the stairs ahead of him. Perhaps now it would finally begin to feel like home. He thought back to a letter his older brother George had written to him when he told him he was building a house. "A home is never complete without a woman in the parlor and the sound of children in the house."

CHAPTER TWO

Jennie lingered in the parlor, running her hand along the smooth wood of the table. It was the same one they owned in Utica, yet here in this new house it seemed different. She wondered if it could be so easy for a life to change in the same way. A new city, a new house, a whole new set of friends—would it make her happy?

This wasn't a change that she had sought. Life in Utica was far from satisfying, but if it had been up to her, she'd have left for somewhere bigger, not a farm town with dirt streets. She had hoped when she married that she had left farm towns behind, but after the troubles in Utica she'd had little choice but to agree to the move.

"Mother! Come see upstairs," Clara called to her, and she turned and climbed the stairs to meet the girls on the upstairs landing.

They were eager to show off the bedrooms down the hallway to the left. They took her hand and led her into the front bedroom. Two windows faced the street, and their double bed was between them.

"Isn't it lovely?" Edna asked, and Jennie nodded with a smile.

The rooms were furnished with beds, wardrobes, and dressers, but little else. There was still much work to be done. There were wall hangings to buy and wallpaper to select before it would begin to look and feel like home. Newt led them across the hallway to the master bedroom, then down the hall to the bath and the third bedroom. The girls were fascinated by the size of the bathtub and the gleaming white porcelain fixtures. A narrow stairway at the back of the house led down to the kitchen.

When they'd explored the entire house, the girls ran off to do it all over again. Jennie and Newt stood together on the back step and looked out at the back yard. The lot was narrow and deep, just thirty feet wide, but it stretched over three hundred feet from the tree-lined street. The neighbor's lilac bushes were in full bloom and the yard radiated green in the bright sunshine.

"It's a bit wild at the moment, but once we hire a gardener, it should shape up nicely," Newt said.

She looked out at the wild, unkempt expanse that seemed to defy taming. Like the house itself, he had left it a blank canvas for her to fill however she pleased. After years of living in a townhouse, it would be good to have some open space again; a quiet place to sit without the prying eyes of the neighborhood upon her.

Fanning herself against the heat, she turned to see him looking at her, his face expressionless as he waited for her to speak. He shifted his eyes, avoiding her gaze. Yes, she thought, he still looks to me for approval. How can a man so unsure of himself succeed in business? she wondered.

"Newt, it will make a lovely home," she assured him, and he seemed relieved. How could she make him know how empty she felt? After eight years of marriage and two children, they were more distant than ever. Sometimes he seemed more at ease in the presence of the children than he did alone with her. Was it her fault?

"Do you really think it will make a difference?" Newt asked.

She looked out at the wild grass growing knee-deep and the lilac bushes so laden with blossoms that they bent near the ground. Why couldn't he understand that just getting out of Utica was freedom enough for her?

"I mean this move. Do you think it will change things between us?"

Jennie paused in silence. They'd had this conversation so many times already there seemed little point in continuing it. The days and the nights she spent alone while he was setting up the factory in Batavia were interminable. A social pariah, she had become nothing more than a madwoman locked in a tower. This move to a small town on the western edge of the state was her only way to escape that corseted prison.

"Come, let's go back inside and get out of this sun," Jennie said, avoiding the question. "The luggage should be arriving soon."

♦

In a little while the wagon arrived carrying their luggage. The workmen carried the steamer trunks upstairs and Jennie set to work unpacking clothes as Newt returned to the factory. The girls unpacked their dolls and played quietly in the parlor, setting up the tea service and pretending to host a party. In its own way the move felt like make-believe to Jennie, too. Unfolding the dresses and hanging them in the wardrobe, she could as easily have been a little girl playing with her dolls. Straightening the petticoats and smoothing the folds in the crinoline, she imagined this home to be nothing but a life-sized dollhouse. Growing up in her parents' house in Clayville, she had always dreamed of having a house of her very own, a brownstone with ivy-covered walls on a bustling street in a big city. When she was six, her father brought her along on a business trip to Albany, where the brick homes stood shoulder to shoulder and the footfalls of hooves echoed along the cobblestone streets. She knew right then that she wanted to live in the city. To live where there was constant motion.

She was nineteen when she first met Newt, and she'd felt as if she would burst if she did not get out of Clayville. He was a bookkeeper at her father's machine shop in Utica when her father brought him home for dinner. On that summer night, Newt's waxed mustache and formal manners made him seem to her the model of a refined city man. He was a grown man of twenty-eight, yet he spoke to her so timidly and tenderly that she felt at times as if he were still a boy. After dinner was over and the dishes were cleared, she heard him on the front porch smoking cigars and discussing business with her father. She stood there in the warm summer darkness listening and wondering what his life in the city must be like. What fun it would be to spend evenings amid the excitement of dinner parties and trips to the theater along gaslit streets. Not at all like her sleepy evenings on the farm, where the only lights were the flickering stars above the fields. Later that night, from the window of her darkened room above the porch, she heard him ask her father if he could return to call on her.

His visits became a weekly occurrence after that. He'd ride out to Clayville each Sunday after church and they would spend the day talking on the porch or walking in the countryside. Walking those dusty roads, she would pick lilies from the bank and bring them home to place in a vase on the dining room table. He would walk beside her, asking about her life and what she hoped to do with it. He spoke little of himself, but seemed content to listen to her talk for hours about her desire to move to the city. How she wanted to live in a large brick home, on paved streets, in a city where the buzz of activity never stopped.

When dinner was over he would excuse himself from the table and put on his coat to leave, then stand on the front step and look into her eyes to ask solemnly if it would be all right for him to visit again the next week. She would giggle, roll her eyes, and say, "If you must."

His sincerity was disarming and amusing. As the weeks passed, she found herself looking forward to his visits. He was more refined and scholarly than the farm boys who had courted her before. Regardless of the weather, he always arrived in a coat and hat with a flower in his lapel. He was quiet, but she commanded every moment of his attention. Even at dinner with her parents, discussing business or the weather, his eyes never seemed to leave her.

Standing on the porch one Sunday evening in spring, as golden blades of sunlight cast long shadows across the field, Newt turned to her and took her hand. He knelt and said, "Jennie, I would like nothing more than for you to marry me. Will you be my wife?"

Looking into his dark, earnest eyes, the only surprise she felt was that it had taken him so long to ask. He moved slowly, for sure, but it had been almost a year since they met. She couldn't do anything for a moment but nod her head, searching for words, until he placed her hand against his mouth and kissed it, his mustache brushing against her skin like the bristles of a horsehair brush.

She laughed, and when he stood, she threw her arms around his shoulders, drawing him close. Watching from behind the lace curtains in the living room, her mother and father stepped out onto the porch to congratulate them. When she woke the next morning, it all seemed like a dream.

They were married in July and moved into a rented house in Utica. Edna was born less than a year later. Motherhood quickly took over Jennie's life as she spent her days taking care of the baby and preparing the house for her husband's return each evening. Her dreams of travel were postponed even further when she became pregnant with Clara just four months after Edna was born. Newt was still a bookkeeper at her father's shop, but was looking for an opportunity to improve their place in life. He took a job working for Mr. Palmer, the father of a childhood friend, and before long had begun to learn the box-making trade. When Newt accompanied Mr. Palmer to New York and Boston for business, Jennie found herself alone with the children in the evenings as well. Her mother was a great help when she needed it, but it wasn't just the work of raising two daughters that taxed her. She had envisioned a life of gay parties in Utica when they were married, but now spent most of her evenings alone. She was starved for lively conversation. Her only companions were a few young mothers in the neighborhood, but all they cared to discuss was the monotonous routine of child rearing.

When she pressed Newt to spend more time at home, he promised it would get better. Just a few more years and Palmer would retire, and then he would buy into the business as a partner with the son. William Palmer had been a friend since childhood, and they had already discussed their plans for the business. The younger Palmer, who was mechanically gifted, was convinced that a fresh investment of capital could double their output. Newt felt that learning the business and making the contacts in large eastern cities would serve him well as a future owner. He promised her that if she could be patient, in a few years' time they would be buying a house of their own and hiring a full-time servant to help with the housework.

Jennie was despondent, but her mother counseled her to be patient. All young couples went through these times, she said, and Newt was a hard worker and a good provider. If she would just wait and see, in a few years they would be moving with the upper class of Utica.

When the elder Palmer died unexpectedly in the winter of 1879, things went as Newt had promised. The money he had saved allowed him to purchase a share of the business.

Soon their income improved and Jennie had money to buy nicer things. Her mother watched the girls while Newt was away so she could head into Albany to shop on State Street. That was where she first met Johnson.

Johnson Lynch was a tall, muscular young man who was fresh from law school on the East Coast. At six foot two with a roguish smile and a thick head of curly brown hair, he'd caught her eye at the few parties Newt took her to. He was the kind of man who stood out in a crowd. Whether he was standing in the bar smoking with the men or sitting at the dinner table making small talk, he was always the center of attention.

Riding on the train to Albany one morning, Jennie

was surprised to see him walk up the aisle and introduce himself. He didn't lack for confidence.

"Good afternoon, dear lady. Please forgive me for bothering you, but would you mind if I had a seat?" he said with a bow.

"No, not at all," Jennie responded, smiling and noticing the deep blue of his eyes as he looked directly into hers. "Does the gentleman have a name, or is he travelling incognito?"

"My apologies! Johnson L. Lynch, at your service," he said, extending a hand.

"Mrs. E. N. Rowell," she answered, putting emphasis on "Mrs." as she placed her hand in his.

"Yes, I know," he said. "I couldn't help but recognize you from the dinner party at Palmer's last month."

"Oh, really? I don't recall seeing you there," she said. "Perhaps you've mistaken me for someone else."

"Oh, no, I am quite sure it was you. I wouldn't forget a face as lovely as yours," Johnson responded.

Jennie blushed, then added, "Oh, yes, you must have been that tall fellow in the parlor playing Liar's Club."

Johnson let out a deep baritone laugh and Jennie noticed the sparkle of his diamond cufflinks reflecting the light from the window.

"Tell me, Mr. Lynch, do you often spend your afternoon on the train accosting women?"

"Yes, I do, but only the beautiful ones," he responded, smiling.

The coach swayed gently as the train snaked along the Mohawk River on its way to Albany. Outside the window, swallows darted above the surface of the river. Swooping and circling in pursuit of each other, their wingtips nearly touched the water.

Jennie and Johnson talked all the way to Albany, where he would attend to court. Jennie imagined his charm would serve him well in front of a jury. When they reached the station, he saw her to a hack and paid her fare. As the carriage pulled away from the curb, he stood watching her leave, then removed his hat and gave her a deep, exaggerated bow. It would be weeks before they crossed paths again, but she couldn't stop thinking about the amusing conversation on the train. She hoped it would not be the last one they had.

♦

Jennie finished emptying the trunks and boxes, then paused in front of the mirror to examine the lines forming around the corners of her eyes. She was twenty-six now, and already she could see a small crease forming beneath her chin. Her clothes told the same tale, no longer fitting as easily as they once had. She couldn't help but feel that her beauty was beginning to fade, like a vase of lilies left too long in the sun. How many more years did she have left before her hair began to gray and men stopped noticing her altogether?

CHAPTER THREE

The evening sun was slanting through the maple trees, leaving long shadows across the dirt street. The mourning doves had already begun their cooing and humidity still weighed heavy in the air, with little breeze to stir the curtains as Newt, Jennie and the girls made their way next door for tea with the Kings.

Hiram and Harriet King were in their early thirties, with only one child, a girl of six. The adults settled in the front parlor drinking tea and eating sandwiches while the girls played in the next room and the housekeeper busied herself in the kitchen. Hiram was a maltster at Fish's Malting House, but the Kings did not seem to want for money. They had lived in their home for almost ten years and were some of the first residents on the street.

"Jennie, tell me about Utica. Will you miss it here in our little village?" Harriet asked.

"Oh, Utica was a nice enough town, but I can't say I will miss it all that much. It was nice to be so close to Albany, though. Tell me, do you get up to Rochester very often?"

"Oh, not so much. We have just about all we need right here," Harriet responded.

Jennie wrinkled her brow and said in a conspiratorial tone, "Yes, I am sure you do. But it is not just needs that make a woman want to visit the city."

Harriet laughed and looked surprised, placing her hand over her mouth. "Yes, I suppose there is more to life than bread and milk," she said, smiling.

Harriet was a slender woman with dark hair and brown eyes. Jennie thought it odd that she had only one child, but did not want to pry so soon after meeting her. She wondered if there had been complications during Harriet's pregnancy, or if the Kings, too, found intimacy difficult after having children.

"Little Jennie is a darling girl," Jennie told Harriet, "and I am not just saying that because she has such a lovely name."

"Thank you," Harriet said. "Sometimes I worry about her becoming lonely, being the only child in the family. I wish she had other siblings to play with, but the Lord decided it just wasn't meant to be. That's why I was so happy to hear that you and Newt had girls almost the same age. I said to Hiram, at last, little Jennie will have some playmates."

"Are there no other children nearby?" Jennie asked.

"Oh, no, there are others," Harriet said. "The Reeds, on the other side of you, have a little boy. It's just that Jennie's cousins are all so much older, and there are mostly little boys in the neighborhood."

Hiram and Newt excused themselves and walked out onto the porch to smoke.

"Tell me about the other folks on the street," Jennie said.

"Well," Harriet began, "John and Helen Reed have only recently moved here from Ohio. They have a daughter of thirteen and a son of seven. Then there is Dr. Showerman and his family. His daughter Mamie is fourteen and has been a wonderful help in watching Jennie for me if I have errands outside of town."

"Oh, that is good to know!" Jennie said. "Perhaps we can ask her to watch the children one afternoon, and you can come with me to Rochester. I have so much to buy for the house. I would appreciate the help."

Harriet lit up at the idea. "Yes, I would love to help, if I can convince Hiram to let me go."

"Oh, Hiram seems like a gentleman. I'm sure he wouldn't want to act un-neighborly," Jennie said.

Harriet filled Jennie in on all the neighbors. It seemed as if every house on Bank Street was owned by a young family. It would be good for the girls to have children their own age to play with, Jennie thought, something that had been lacking in Utica.

Outside on the porch, Hiram and Newt were puffing on their cigars in the evening light, discussing the business of the village. The shadows lengthened and birds called out from the higher branches of the trees. Lights began to flicker on in the parlor windows and front porches were peopled with silent figures taking in the evening air. Downtown, the lamplighter worked his way down Main Street lighting the gas lights. The whole city seemed to be robed in silence as Jennie and Harriet came out onto the porch and called for the children.

They gathered up the kids and exchanged goodnights. Walking back home, Jennie reached out and held Newt's hand. "They seem like nice people," she said when she was certain to be out of hearing.

"I was pleased to see you making friends with Harriet. It will be good for you to have a woman to talk to when I'm travelling," Newt said, placing a subtle emphasis on "woman" that Jennie did not appreciate.

"Perhaps if you were around more, it would not be such a necessity. I don't understand why Palmer can't go on some of these trips and leave you behind to watch the factory."

"Jennie, I've explained this before. It's best if Palmer stays in the shop to manage production and I'm the one to call on our customers."

"Will it always be?" Jennie asked. "Why can't you hire someone else to do that for you?"

"We can't afford it at the moment, but I promise, as soon as we can I'll add a salesman."

Jennie shooed the girls upstairs to get ready for bed while Newt lit the oil lamps in the parlor. The light flickered and danced upon the ceiling, the colored lamp shade casting hues of red and yellow on the room. The smell of fresh varnish still hung in the air when it was hot, the new home breathing like a living creature.

She had told him that her relationship with the young lawyer was platonic, and he'd said he believed her, but the impropriety of a young married woman walking around town with a bachelor was all the evidence the scolds and wags of Utica had needed. Rumors soon spread about the frequency of Johnson Lynch's calls on the Rowell house while Newt was away. Perhaps she was naïve not to expect it, but she could not resist his company. Once the rumors began to circulate, she'd become defiant and only more emboldened to be seen with him in public. In her opinion, it was her defiance more than her visits with Johnson that upset everyone.

After she put the girls to bed, Jennie descended by the back stairs to avoid Newt, who sat reading in the parlor. She stepped out onto the back porch and stood there in the darkness listening to the crickets. Would the distance really help her forget about Johnson? Did she even want to? She wondered what he was doing at that very moment. In the deep shadows of the yard, lightning bugs began to blink on and off like so many signal fires. She wondered what message they were sending her.

CHAPTER FOUR

From the window of his third-floor office, Newt Rowell looked out over the wagons and carriages moving down the dusty Main Street. In the middle of the day the village was alive with activity. The whistle of a train leaving the station echoed off the brick buildings and made his heart speed up. It wasn't the frontier, but there was a sense of newness in the air that inspired him about Batavia. The town was a crossroads, crisscrossed with tracks like iron veins on the back of a hand. Long before the railroads were built there, the Iroquois Nation beat footpaths through the woods. By the muddy banks of the Tonawanda Creek, the trails from the Genesee Valley crossed the trails leading to Lakes Erie and Ontario.

There along the great bend where the creek turned toward the west was a grassy clearing in the midst of the virgin forest. When colonists began to move west of the Catskills they followed these Indian footpaths, clearing the trees and widening the trails until they became roads. At their junction, just steps from the banks of the creek, stood the stately gray limestone courthouse with its cupola rising above all, like an axis around which the town revolved.

Batavia was soon the largest town in this part of the state, but the ground was too high, and when the canal was dug from Buffalo to Albany it passed through the swamps and muck lands to the north. For a while it seemed as if the village would fade and become a sleepy backwater on a shallow, unnavigable creek. But the same geography that had made it the natural crossroads for the Seneca saved it. When the first tracks were laid in western New York, they followed the same valleys and firm soil as the natives' footpaths.

It was railroads that saved the town, and it was railroads that brought Newt and Palmer there from Utica. From the station in Batavia a traveler could be in New York, Boston, Cleveland, Chicago, or Ontario in a day. From this central point they could call on companies all over the Northeast and ship boxes and cartons to the heart of North America's industry. Each week a new factory seemed to rise somewhere along the tracks. Ploughs, guns, harvesters; the tools of westward expansion were forged along those tracks and shipped west to tame the prairie. To a person building a business, it seemed as if anything was possible.

As he sat at his desk, Newt thought about the other reason they'd moved the business to Batavia.

His marriage to Jennie had begun with the usual nervous excitement, and the wedding was quickly followed by children. He'd worked hard to provide a home for their burgeoning family, but he knew it wasn't easy on Jennie. Soon she was alone with two small children as he traveled with the elder Palmer and learned the box-making business. In retrospect, he saw that he should have been more attentive to her needs, but he'd had trouble making her understand that his time away from home was for the good of the family.

When the elder Palmer died and he bought into the business, things began to improve. Soon, the associations Newt began to make among the young professionals in Utica led to new opportunities. There were invitations to parties and social events. Even though he wanted to fade into the wallpaper at these events, it heartened him to see Jennie excited. Unlike him, she was in her natural element in a crowd. She sparkled like a chandelier when others were around. He was content to stand in the shadows and watch her float from group to group, talking and laughing with ease. Her beauty was undeniable. When she entered a room the men stopped their discussions and she became the focus of attention. It gave him a thrill to see how they looked at her, knowing that she belonged to him.

Soon rumors about her flirtatiousness began to circulate. Perhaps it was the jealousy of the older women, as Jennie insisted, but he couldn't help but wonder if there was some truth to the rumors. Eventually he didn't know what to believe. There was no denying that certain men seemed to find their way into her path time and again. When he returned from a trip one evening, Palmer pulled him aside and informed him that he'd seen Jennie strolling the shaded streets on the arm of a young lawyer during the afternoons. When Newt brought it up to his wife, she did not deny it. Instead, she seemed injured by his distrust, and in the end he felt sorry for not believing her. She claimed that the man was a dear friend, someone she felt she could speak to when Newt was away. She swore it was nothing more than companionship that she sought.

But the rumors persisted until the Rowells were no longer welcome in society. Invitations were mysteriously lost, and when Newt and Jennie did appear, the silence that greeted them was unnerving. It began to tear at Jennie to be so isolated, where once she had been the center of attention. She began to spend more time with Johnson Lynch, the young lawyer, and became more brazen about being seen in public, until the whispers behind Newt's back became too much for him to stand.

This move to Batavia would be a fresh start and a chance for the Rowells to reinvent themselves. They had no history here, and Newt hoped that whatever had happened in Utica could finally be forgotten. A new village, a new house, and new acquaintances; everything would be different here. Already business was increasing, and Palmer agreed that the new location was already paying dividends.

A breeze from the open window rustled the papers on Newt's desk and brought some relief from the heat. He stood and left the office to look in on the factory. The production room was on the top floor where skylights provided light and ventilation, but the breeze Newt had felt in his office was absent here. Newt wiped the sweat from his brow as he crossed the room to where Palmer was adjusting machinery. Women were removing cut pieces of cardboard from the feeder, screen-printing them, and folding them into packing crates. Their small hands were well suited to handling the delicate pillboxes, and Newt found them to be more conscientious workers than the men.

"How's it coming?" Newt asked as Palmer adjusted a cutting blade with a wrench.

"I think I've got it figured out," Palmer responded. His starched white shirt was soaked with sweat and sticking to the center of his back. "This infernal heat must have expanded the tension rods and made the blades slide loose." Palmer rolled his sleeves down and walked across the room to speak with the women.

"That's it, girls. We've got three more crates to fill to complete this order. Keep an eye on those cut lines, and let me know if anything changes." Picking up his coat, he followed Newt back to the front office.

"The Lilly order will be ready to go tomorrow, so you can go ahead and arrange the shipment," Palmer told Newt.

"Four shipments this week already," Newt observed. "If we keep up at this pace, we might have to hire an office girl."

"Why, have you spotted a pretty one I might be interested in?" Palmer joked, winking at Newt from behind his glasses.

They had known each other since they were children, having grown up just a few doors apart. Newt's brother George had left home when Newt was still a boy, and Newt had been a sickly child, often confined to the porch while the other children ran about the neighborhood. For some reason Newt never understood, Palmer began dropping by to sit on the front steps and entertain him with grandiose stories and tall tales. Perhaps he needed an audience as much as Newt needed a friend. Naturally quiet, and shy in the company of other children, Newt came to rely on the tall and handsome Palmer to be his connection to the world around him, and Palmer became like a second brother.

When he bought into the box business after Palmer's father died, Newt was concerned that it would create tension between them, but they found that their personalities and skills complemented each other well. While Newt spent most of his time keeping the books or calling on drug manufacturers, Palmer spent his time working on the equipment or giving directions on the shop floor.

"I trust that the trip went well, and your family has arrived?" asked Palmer as they entered the office.

"Yes," Newt answered, taking his seat. "The children were excited about the move."

"And Jennie?"

Newt was silent for a moment, then answered, "Yes, I think Jennie will appreciate the move, too."

Palmer removed his glasses and wiped his face with a handkerchief.

"Newt, you know how I feel about the situation," he said. "I can't stand to see her make a fool out of you again."

"It wasn't her fault," Newt replied quickly.

"I know Lynch is a scoundrel, but you cannot place the blame solely on him."

"I don't," Newt answered. "I place the blame on myself. If I had paid more attention to her needs, it never would have happened."

"Newt, she should have never let it get to that point."

"I don't want to have this discussion again," Newt said, slamming his hand onto his desk. "He seduced her, and we have put it behind us. It will not happen again."

Palmer paused, then placed his glasses back on his face. "Newt. I am only telling you this as your oldest and closest friend. I don't want to see you mocked behind your back here as you were in Utica. That's why I suggested this move. That's why I have supported you throughout this. All I ask is that you not be naïve."

Newt closed his eyes against the memory of his humiliation, then nodded in silent agreement.

CHAPTER FIVE

Life quickly settled into routine at home. The girls were quick to make friends and spent their days playing in the garden and on the rope swing in the Kings' yard. Jennie found a girl down the street to help with the children as she busied herself shopping for furnishings for the new house. In the evenings when Newt was away, she would gossip on the back porch with Harriet King while the children played in the yard.

By mid-September, the heat of summer had finally broken. The rains came hard, turning the streets to mud and revealing leaks in the roof. Jennie directed the workmen as they tarred the leaking seams and joints. Gas lines were being laid down Bank Street that autumn, and the children watched in fascination as men with shovels and pickaxes dug the trenches.

Jennie did her part to make the new house seem

more like a home. When she wasn't taking care of the girls or the housework, she found time to paint and hang wallpaper. It was dirty and messy work, but she felt a sense of pride when she was done. One by one the rooms were transformed, until each one bore her imprint.

Newt did his best to help, but his long hours meant that the bulk of the work fell to her. When he returned home for supper, he showed signs of wear she hadn't seen since he first went to work for Palmer's father. Despite his assurances, they had yet to make a trip to Rochester.

Autumn in western New York was a kaleidoscope of color as the maples flared orange, red, and yellow and the fields turned golden brown. The farmers brought in their harvest and the streets bustled with wagons. The weather turned colder and the days grew shorter, but to Jennie they seemed to last forever.

During the evenings she and Newt sat in the parlor and read by the light of the oil lamps while the children played and the clock slowly counted off the hours.

One night in September, Jennie set down her book. "Newt, I've been wanting to go to Rochester and shop for winter coats for the girls. Do you think we could go this weekend?"

Newt paused and looked up from his newspaper. "Hmm . . . I'm afraid this weekend won't be a good time. Palmer and I are planning to make some changes to the machines."

Jennie sighed heavily. "When will be a good time, Newt? When the children have pneumonia from wearing their summer clothes in the snow?"

"Now, Jennie, why must you go to Rochester to buy clothes? What's wrong with the clothes at Gould and Town's?"

"You wouldn't understand."

Newt sat up in his chair, folding his newspaper. "Well, tell me, then, so I can understand."

"The clothes in the stores here are fine, if you're a farmer's daughter," Jennie answered. "But you won't see the children on East Main Street wearing them. When the girls start school I don't want anyone looking down their noses at them."

Puzzled, Newt asked, "Why should anyone look down upon the children? They aren't barefoot Colleens from the South Side."

"Newt, you can be so naïve. The people in this town are very aware of everyone's place in the pecking order. Trust me, the teacher will take one look at the children and know where their parents stand. If you want the girls treated like farmers, that's fine, but I prefer they be able to look the pastor's children in the eye."

Newt picked up his paper again. "I am sorry, my dear, but I think you are making too much of this."

"Perhaps I'll just have to take the girls myself, then," Jennie said as he unfolded his paper and began reading.

She listened to the girls playing with their dollhouse in the next room and wondered how a man so intent on bettering himself could be so blind to the social order. It was apparent to her the first time they walked up the steps of First Baptist Church that they were being judged. Sitting in the vaulted interior, fanning herself against the heat, she could feel everyone's eyes on them and imagined the whispered conversations that would start once the service was over.

How could Newt not see it? Perhaps the men he encountered were only interested in the money they made, but she knew their wives paid attention to where it came from, how one dressed and on which street they lived. Bank Street may not have been the best street in town, but it was far from the wrong side of the tracks. Most of the families were headed by young businessmen and professionals. They may not have hired help in the kitchen, but they carried themselves with the assurance that they would soon.

Jennie left the room, calling to the girls that it was time for bed. If Newt would not take her shopping to Rochester, or give her the money to do so, she would have to find another way. Until then it would do little good to argue with him. It was easier to move a mountain than to get him to change his ways.

She put the children to bed, then undressed and sat in front of the mirror to let down her hair. Undoing the pins, she let her long blonde locks fall down around her shoulders. They shone in the lamplight, betraying none of the gray hairs the harsh light of day revealed. Running the brush through her hair, she looked at the shadows across her face and wondered if Johnson still thought of her. Surely he had forgotten her and taken to chasing someone else around the parlors of Utica and Albany. Why couldn't she forget him?

She climbed into bed and turned out the light, but sleep was elusive. Lying on her side with her back to the door, she heard Newt climbing the steps and closing the bathroom door. In a few minutes he climbed in beside her and reached out to touch her arm. Feigning sleep, she rolled away from him and closed her eyes. She could hear him sigh as he lay back on his pillow, and she waited. Before long his breathing slowed and he was asleep.

In the long shadows of the room, she imagined Johnson looming over her, bending down to kiss her. She tried to remember his touch. The roughness of his hands, and the way he placed them on the small of her back and lifted her up to meet his mouth, the bristle of his mustache against her face, the wet eagerness of his kisses.

Outside, the wind rustled through the trees and the dry leaves crackled like kindling about to burst into flame. She rolled over and closed her eyes.

CHAPTER SIX

The woolen clouds pressed down upon the village, scudding past in an unending blanket of gray. The few leaves that still clung to the branches twisted in the wind. Jennie closed the front door behind her and stepped down from the porch. The girls would be in school for another three hours before she had to meet them on the corner. With her handbag over her arm, she set off towards Main Street.

The breath of passing horses rose like clouds of steam in the cold air. The awnings were drawn up along the storefronts to let in what little sunlight might filter through the overcast. Slowly Jennie made the rounds of the stores on her errands.

It may not have been State Street in Albany, but Newt was right, the shops had everything she needed. What they lacked in fashion they made up for with practicality. The house was coming together. The painting and decorating were complete, and she had chosen furniture for all of the rooms. The price was dear, but business was good at the box factory and their credit at the stores was never in doubt.

Now that winter was coming and the girls were in school, she had less and less to do during the afternoons. Aside from having tea with Harriet, she had little interaction with her neighbors. Part of the problem was Newt, who was often traveling on business, and when they did go to parties he tended to disappear into another room to talk business with the men. Crossing the street, she stepped down into a puddle, splashing the hem of her yellow dress with mud. How nice it would be, she thought, to live somewhere she wasn't constantly washing dirt and muck from their clothes. She envied Newt's travels and wondered what it must be like in New York, or Boston or Chicago, cities bustling with crowds and alive with energy.

She entered Lorish's grocery to look over the produce, then arranged to have her order delivered and stopped at Kenyon's to buy coffee and tea. On her way out the door, she noticed a set of stationery in the window. She paused, then went back inside and bought it.

When she got home she set the stationery on the desk in the parlor and pulled out a sheet of paper. She rubbed her fingers over the parchment, feeling its grain and weight. She picked up a pen and began to write.

Dearest Johnson,

It has been a long time since we last saw each other. Much has happened, and I regret all the troubles that resulted. As you know, we have moved west to Batavia for Newt's business. We have built a house of our own, and I have been busy taking care of the girls and making this new place into a warm home for them. The move has not been an easy one. This is a nice enough village, but a tad sleepy and remote, and I miss the social life of Utica. I have not met a friend whom I could trust as much as I do you.

I am sure you are surprised to find a letter from me. I wanted to write you, to say that I miss our times together and hope that you recall them as fondly as I do.

With warmest regards,

Jennie

As she finished the letter, Jennie's hands began to shake and she felt a flutter of excitement in her heart. It was foolish of her to be afraid of being found out. Alone in the house, with Newt half a continent away, she had nothing to fear. Looking up at the clock, she realized it was time to meet the girls, so she quickly folded the letter and placed it in her jacket pocket. She would have to wait to mail it.

Walking to meet the children, she could feel the letter against her breast, and wondered how Johnson would feel to know she'd held it so close. Would he hold it to his face and smell her scent? The very thought excited her and her face began to flush.

That night after the children were in bed, she carried the letter to her bedroom and rubbed it with perfume before sealing the envelope.

CHAPTER SEVEN

Newt looked out the window of the gently swaying coach as the brown fields of northern Ohio rolled by in unending succession. The red barns stood out like bloodstains against the gray and colorless landscape. Newt was lost in thought.

Business had been improving since the move to Batavia, and it wasn't just the cheap labor and better access to western markets. Newt had talked Palmer into focusing on makers of patent medicine, because pillboxes were smaller and less costly than the larger cartons that were the core of their business in Utica. For one, the pillboxes were more difficult to make, so by specializing in one small market, they were able to set themselves apart from the many box factories springing up across the west. Furthermore, patent medicine makers could afford to pay more for packaging. By putting extra effort into design, Newt had been able to improve the company's profit margins.

Of course, nothing would have been possible without Palmer, who had a knack for design. His packages had a flair that appealed to medicine companies seeking to make their products stand out on crowded drugstore shelves. So long as they were able to keep producing creative designs, there seemed to be no limit to the potential. As soon as one company put its products into a Rowell & Palmer-designed box, its competitors wanted to follow suit.

Newt began to turn the numbers over in his mind, calculating the number of boxes per account that could be possible and comparing it to the output of their factory. He reckoned that before the next summer they would need to move to a larger space. He had already begun discussions with the owner of the building next door about taking over the adjacent floor. It would be simple enough to knock a hole in the wall to connect the two buildings and double their production space. All they needed to do was agree on a price.

Outside the train, the failing light of late afternoon cast a rose-pink glow upon the clouds. Already the sky in the east was turning a deeper shade of blue as the train sped toward Chicago. By morning he would be there. It was impressive to behold the tall buildings springing skyward, and hard to believe that only ten years earlier the city had been reduced to ashes. Had a phoenix ever risen as quickly or as high as Chicago had?

He thought of Jennie, and how she would love to

see a city like this. Perhaps he should take some time off next year to take her and the children along. Maybe Chicago would be the phoenix that could bring their love back from the ashes.

He'd hoped things would be better in Batavia, and for a while they had, but it was clear to him that Jennie was restless. Her requests to go places and buy nicer things had only grown since summer. How much longer would she be content on the dusty streets of their village? He had been avoiding the social scene in Batavia, but perhaps he owed it to his wife to attend a few more parties or join a club. Palmer had joined the Batavia Club to make business contacts, and the cost of membership posed no problem for Newt. If he were honest with himself, he would have confessed that his reluctance to join was a result of the troubles in Utica. He knew that eventually he had to start trusting Jennie again if they were going to put the past behind them. As darkness fell outside, he rose and headed to the dining car to take his supper.

CHAPTER EIGHT

More than a week had passed since she mailed the letter, and each day Jennie held her breath as she stopped at the post office. Would this be the day she would get a response? Maybe he had given up on her and moved on to a younger, more accessible woman. She felt even more isolated now that winter had come and Newt was travelling again. What she wouldn't give to have Johnson's company and conversation to pass the hours.

The day she opened the postal box and saw a letter addressed to her without a return address, her heart leapt. She pushed it into her handbag and rushed home to open it in private, smiling when she slid out a letter in Johnson's handwriting.

Dearest Jennie,
How wonderful it is to hear from you again. You write as if

Thomas Gahr

you were afraid I forgot you, but nothing could be further from the truth. Ever since you left the joy has gone out of this town. Walking the streets where we once shared such gay conversation is almost too much to bear. I feel like your ghost haunts me wherever I go, and I look through the faces at every party, hoping against hope to see your lovely visage once more.

I am both heartened and saddened to hear that you fondly recall our times together. I should very much like to see you again one day. Should you ever return to Utica, please look me up. Until that day I will have to find sustenance in your letters.

With all my love,
Johnson

Jennie read the letter with tears of sorrow and joy. She carried it with her for the rest of the day, pausing to reread it and pore over each word every few minutes. Finally, she took it upstairs and placed it in the drawer of her vanity.

As she was washing the dinner dishes, she heard the front door open and Newt calling out to the girls. Edna and Clara's footsteps echoed down the hallway as they ran to greet him. Wiping her hands on her apron, Jennie walked down the hall to see him kneeling with a girl in each arm as their hands searched his pockets.

"What did you bring us?" Edna cried.

"Why, what makes you think I brought you anything?" Newt answered with furrowed brows.

"Oh, Daddy, you always do."

"Here it is!" Clara shrieked, pulling a small metal bird out of his overcoat.

"What is it?" Edna asked.

"It's a bird, silly," Newt said.

"But what does it do?"

"Wind it up and see."

Newt took the bird, wound the key in its back, and placed it on the floor. With a buzz and a click it came to life, opening and closing its beak. The girls laughed as it chirped and Jennie couldn't help but smile.

"Wherever did you find it?" she asked.

"I bought it from a German street vendor in Chicago. I probably paid too much, but I thought the girls would have a good laugh out of it."

"Well, Mr. Rowell, did you bring me anything?" Jennie asked.

Blushing, Newt mumbled a few words about being in a hurry to make the train.

With a teasing pout on her face, Jennie turned and said, "Well, then, I don't feel so badly about not saving you any supper."

Newt crossed the room and awkwardly reached out to embrace her from behind. His face brushed against her hair and he kissed the back of her neck. "I missed you, Jennie."

Jennie could smell the coal smoke from the train still clinging to his overcoat. It was a smell of travel and faraway places, and she envied him for it.

"What was Chicago like?" she asked.

"It's a marvelous city, and each time I see it I'm amazed by how much it's grown. They have buildings there that reach halfway to the clouds."

She tried to picture it in her mind, the tall stone buildings rising like cliffs above streets teeming with people.

Taking off his coat and hanging it in the hallway, Newt said, "Jennie, I've been thinking, and I've decided to join the Batavia Club. I think it would be a good way for us to meet people and start making some acquaintances."

She turned back to him. "But you loathe parties and socials."

"Yes, but I know they are important for you, and I feel bad when I'm out of town and I think of you here with no one to talk to."

The girls took turns winding the mechanical bird and listening to it chirp for the rest of the evening. Jennie and Newt sat in the parlor and she told him everything that had happened while he was gone. He sat across from her, nodding as she spoke, looking at her with an intensity she had not seen in a long time.

Later that night after the children were asleep, they went upstairs together. As Jennie sat before the mirror in her nightgown, brushing her hair, she sensed Newt's eyes upon her. She realized that the light from the lamp on the vanity shone through the silk of her nightgown, revealing the curve of her breasts. His eyes met her gaze in the mirror, and she smiled at him.

"Mr. Rowell, I do believe you are having impure thoughts about me," she teased.

Placing her brush on the vanity, she reached over and turned out the lamp. Newt crossed the room and put his hands on her shoulders, turning her around. She was surprised by the strength of his grip as he pulled her towards him. Tilting her head, she barely opened her mouth in time to meet his kiss.

He pulled her over to the bed and pressed her down on her back, then removed his clothes and lay down on top of her. Jennie closed her eyes and tried to picture Johnson above her. She reached up and wrapped her arms around her husband's neck as he lifted her nightgown to her hips.

Newt's breath quickened and his shoulders pressed against her face until she had to turn her head to breathe. His hip bones were pressing against her abdomen like a whalebone corset. With a grunt and a stifled cry, he trembled and came to a stop.

She sighed and lay still as he rolled over onto the bed and stood up. Opening her eyes, she could see his silhouette in the darkness as he left the room. A chill ran over her body, and she reached out and pulled the covers over her.

Come Monday, he would be gone again, yet now she felt more alone than ever. In her mind she began composing her next letter to Johnson.

CHAPTER NINE

The letters continued to arrive throughout the winter and into the spring. Jennie found herself looking forward to them. They never failed to make her laugh, or smile, and she adored the attention he paid to her comments. Not a thing she wrote to him went unnoted in his responses.

As summer approached, Newt finally relented and gave her money for a shopping trip. She spent an afternoon window-shopping in Rochester while Harriet watched the children, but she set aside the money for later. All winter long she had been saving whatever she could in the hope of buying a ticket to see Johnson. Now she had more than enough to set her plans into motion.

When Newt announced a trip to Boston and Hartford the following week, she wrote to Johnson and asked him to meet her in Rochester. The days she spent waiting for his reply were excruciating.

Dearest Jennie,

If you only knew how much I long to see you again, you would scarcely believe it. This winter has lasted an eternity, as I have been shuttling between Utica and Albany for cases. Each time I ride that train I think of that lovely spring morning when we met, and how radiant you were. How appropriate that we should finally meet again once the snow has gone and the lilacs are blooming.

I will be at the Powers Hotel next Tuesday at noon. Meet me there, and be certain not to use your real name when signing the register. Travelling lawyers will not attract suspicion as easily as the wives of local businessmen. I will wait for you in the rotunda.

All my love,
Johnson

The following Monday evening she arranged for the children to stay overnight with Harriet, telling her she had to visit a sick relative. In the morning she packed a small valise, and after putting on her finest blue taffeta skirt with a fitted jacket and a small bonnet, she left for the station.

She boarded the 10:15 train, took a seat by the window, and looked out at the village. It had been nearly a year since she arrived in Batavia, and this was her first trip away. It seemed hard to believe that it was over two years since they met.

The train lurched forward and began to move,

picking up speed as it rolled past the burgeoning factories and out into the countryside. As it descended the escarpment, she could see far off into the distance. The sun shone brightly over the patchwork fields and fresh green shoots glowed in the morning light. The hills rolled away into the distance, dotted with the outlines of red barns and emerald woods. Jennie had forgotten how beautiful the country could be. The rush of air through the open window of the coach felt like the cool waters of a lake on a hot summer day.

The train wound its way across the landscape, veering north and east towards the great lake and the city. The thrill of escape brought goose bumps to her arms. How lucky Newt was to be able to cross the country by train, seeing landscapes and cities she'd only dreamed about.

As the train approached Rochester, Jennie could see smoke rising from the mills and factories along the Genesee. Slowing as it entered the city, the train passed through neighborhoods and rows of warehouses before crowds of people appeared, walking the city streets between rising walls of masonry and brick.

Passing between the downtown on the right and the mills on the left, the train crossed the bridge over the Genesee River and pulled into New York Central Station. Stepping out of the station into a district of breweries and clothing factories, Jennie considered hailing a cab, but decided to walk the bustling streets. The morning sun was high and the day was quickly warming up, but it was a pleasant walk. The sidewalks were crowded with people and the streets were full of carriages and horse-drawn trolleys.

Jennie walked five blocks south on St. Paul Street before turning west onto Main Street. There across the bridge was the heart of the city, the department stores, shops, and office buildings that were dominated by the great mansard roof of the Powers Building that rose like a wedding cake at the corner of State and Main. Crossing the river, she could see the great aqueduct of the Erie Canal to her left, with canal boats and barges crossing above the river. To her right she could see the mist of the high falls rising like smoke above the mills, the sound of water drowned out by the locomotives and factories.

She paused in the shade of the awnings to look into the shop windows. Newsboys stood on the corners selling morning papers as she crossed State Street and continued on to the hotel. Walking into the cool shade of the marbled lobby, it took a few moments for her eyes to adjust. The building was brand new and still smelled of varnish and floor polish. Pink marble columns rose to the ceiling, reflecting the yellow incandescence of the globes of electric lights, the first ones she had ever seen.

She made her way to the mahogany desk and rented a room, signing the register as Mrs. E. N. Potter. A bellboy carried her valise and led her across the rotunda and up a wide marble staircase to her room. When he opened the door to her room, she was taken by its opulence. An oriental rug in deep red covered the floor and the furniture gleamed. Plush down pillows adorned the bed and velvet drapes were tied back at the windows to let in the streaming sunlight. It was the kind of hotel room she had dreamed about. She unpacked her bag and freshened up in the cool, white-tiled confines of the separate bath. She looked at her watch; it was 11:30 a.m.

As Jennie started down the stairs into the lobby, she saw Johnson on the round sofa at the center of the room, his hat in his hands resting upon his walking stick, a white flower in the buttonhole of his lapel. He stood as soon as he saw her and walked across the room to meet her at the bottom of the steps. Taking her hand, he kissed it and asked, "How is it possible that you are even more beautiful now than the day I met you?"

"Well, Mr. Lynch, I see you are as good a liar as you have always been, and I thank you for it."

"My God, but it is good to see you again," he said as he looked into her eyes.

"I can't believe it has been so long," she told him. "Seeing you now, I feel as if you have been with me all the time."

Indeed, she thought, he had been there in her heart throughout the long months of separation. How else could she explain his presence in her room those nights when the bed was so empty and cold?

"I trust that you have found the accommodations to your liking?"

"Of course! What's not to love? There can't be a finer hotel in all the country. Although I should even find a barn agreeable if you were in it."

Extending his arm, he said, "Come, let me show you the rest of the city."

Jennie took his arm and they stepped into the bright sunlight of the street. Arm in arm they strolled through the crowds on the sidewalk, absorbed in conversation. Johnson seldom took his eyes off of her and seemed to be hanging on her every word. They stopped for dinner in a restaurant full with the business crowd, and she felt like the center of attention. The eyes of all the men seemed to be on her as she talked and laughed.

Leaning across the table, Johnson whispered, "You have no idea how difficult it is to be this close to you and not be able to hold you in my arms."

Jennie blushed and felt a tingle of excitement as she glanced around to see if anyone had heard him.

"Let me take you back to the hotel," he said, "where I can kiss you without worrying about prying eyes."

"Why, Mr. Lynch," she responded, "you will have to wait until after dinner before you can have your dessert." She fluttered her eyelids, feeling the thrill of the power she had over him.

Climbing the stairs to her room, she glanced back to make sure they were not being followed. Even now, in a city where they were both strangers, she couldn't help but feel as if she was being watched, and the feeling only made the moment more exciting.

As soon as they entered the room, Johnson turned her to him, and bending down, kissed her full on the lips. She put her hands around the bulk of his shoulders and he lifted her feet from the floor with his strong embrace. Kissing passionately, they pulled and tugged at each other's clothes until there was nothing between them. He carried her to the bed and laid her down.

The breeze from the window stirred the drapes and light shone in shafts across the floor. Outside, the noise of the streets echoed between the buildings, but all Jennie could hear was the sound of their breathing as they rolled about on the sheets, Johnson's strong hands at the small of her back as he rolled her on top of him. Her hair fell in a wild tangle about his face, and still they kissed, heedless of the world around them.

They made love again and again, stopping only when the sunlight faded and darkness crept from the corners of the room. She spent the night sleeping with his arm draped across her shoulders like a blanket, the sheets pulled down and the evening air cool against her skin.

When morning came, she woke to his soft kisses on her neck. They made love again, then lay in each other's arms, looking up at the ceiling.

"My dear, the thought of leaving is like a knife blade in my heart," she told him, tears welling in her eyes.

"Shh . . ." he consoled her, "we may be parting for the moment, but it will not be forever."

"I wish we could be together like this every night," she said. "I feel as if I am only alive when we are together, and all the rest is just a dream."

He said nothing, but turned her face towards him and kissed her on the lips.

"Jennie, as much as we want it, it cannot be. You must get back to your life, and your home. I will carry you with me in my heart until we see each other again."

She closed her eyes and wept quietly against his chest.

CHAPTER TEN

"Newt, can you give me a hand?" Jennie called, standing in front of her vanity in a sage-green gown.

"Yes, dear, what is it?" asked Newt, fastening his tie as he entered the room.

"Would you please help with these clasps?" she asked, turning her back to him.

Outside, the rumble of distant thunder rolled through heavy air.

"Oh, I do hope the rain holds off until we get to the party."

She looked at herself in the mirror as he fastened the back of her dress and was struck by her thinness. Her bustled and corseted figure made her look again like the girl that stood on that porch in Clayville the night he proposed.

"You look wonderful, dear," Newt told her.

Smiling at him in the mirror, she answered, "It is

so nice to have a reason to again."

There was a knock at the front door.

"Oh, good, that must be Mamie," Jennie said. "Perhaps we can leave before the rain comes." She went downstairs to answer the door and welcome the girl inside. As she led her through the house giving her instructions, Newt fetched his umbrella from the stand and put on his hat.

When Jennie returned to the entryway, she placed her shawl around her shoulders and they stepped out into the evening air. Ellicott Hall was only four blocks away and the flashes of lightning were still far off to the west. Walking briskly, they turned the corner onto Washington Avenue and continued on to State Street. By the time they reached the front steps of the old clapboard meeting hall, the first few drops of rain had begun to fall, melting dark holes in the dust of the street.

Newt checked his hat and umbrella at the door as Jennie entered the hall. Already a crowd had gathered along the bar at the side of the large assembly room and a small orchestra was setting up in the rear of the hall. This was the first big social they'd attended since Newt joined the Batavia Club, and Jennie was scanning the crowd for familiar faces.

"Oh, look, there are the Kings," she said, nodding towards a table by the dance floor. Harriet waved her hand for them to join them.

"Why, Jennie, you look absolutely lovely," Harriet said as they approached.

"Oh, thank you," Jennie answered. "It's amazing I was able to do anything with my hair in this awful humidity."

Hiram nodded at Newt, asking, "How is the box business doing, Newt?"

"Good, good. And you?"

"Oh, I can't complain. Weather like this is good for my business, keeps the taverns busy and the breweries running."

"Hmm . . . yes, I suppose," said Newt distractedly as his eyes searched the room.

Looking around, Jennie said, "What a large social. I feel like I don't know a soul here. Harriet, you'll have to introduce me and tell me who's here."

"Pardon me, dear, I see someone I need to speak to," Newt said, excusing himself.

Looking at Jennie, Harriet asked, "Is something wrong?"

Jennie smiled a terse smile and answered, "I'm afraid you'll have to excuse us. Newt isn't very comfortable at parties and seems to forget his manners. I'm sure he'll be right back."

Glancing over in the direction of the bar, she saw Palmer talking animatedly with a circle of men.

"Oh, I see, there's his business partner, Mr. Palmer. I should have known he wouldn't be able to go an evening without talking business."

"Oh, no need to apologize, Jennie, dear," Harriet said. "All men are like that. I am sure Hiram will spend half the evening holed up in a corner talking business." She smiled at Hiram, who seemed lost in thought. "Won't you, Hiram?"

"Hmm, sorry? What was that you said, dear?"

Jennie and Harriet laughed. "See?" said Harriet.

"They're all the same."

Hiram shrugged and followed Newt to the bar.

"Well, Harriet, I must disagree. Not all men are more interested in business than lovely women," Jennie teased.

"Perhaps, but I have yet to meet one."

"Well then, perhaps someday I'll have the chance to introduce you to one."

"Who might this mystery man be?"

"Oh, just a dear friend of mine from Utica. He's a veritable prince charming when it comes to the ladies. Perhaps I should be careful, though, or he might just steal you away from poor old Hiram," Jennie teased.

"Oh, I'm afraid 'poor old Hiram' has nothing to worry about. One man is just about all the headache I can manage anymore."

"Oh, dear, don't underestimate yourself. I'm sure you managed quite a string of suitors before you chose Hiram."

Harriet laughed. "Well, let's just say that I haven't been too disappointed in my choice, although there are some days when I wonder what I was thinking."

"Yes, I know what you mean," Jennie said. "If only I had known that the effort Newt put into courting me would end up being just another business proposition."

"Oh, surely you don't mean that," Harriet implored.

"I'm afraid I do. Things have not been well between us for quite some time. He seems far more interested in business ventures than he is in his wife."

"Come now," Harriet said. "He surely must see

how lucky he is to have a wife like you."

"If he does, he never shows it," Jennie said. "Some days I feel like just another account that he attends to when he must."

"I'm not sure I would be able to cope with such behavior," said Harriet.

"Oh, there are many ways to cope," Jennie said coyly.

She looked across the room to where Newt and Palmer were talking among a group of men. How strange a breed they were, Jennie thought. She had seen many men like them in Utica. Men that seemed to move in a world entirely separate from those of their wives and children. That was what always set Johnson apart from the others. No matter who was in the room, when she was with him she felt like she was the center of the universe. It was hard to believe Newt had ever made her feel that way. They had been together for seven years already, but it seemed like a lifetime ago when he came calling for her. What a ridiculous girl she had been.

Lightning flashed outside the windows and was quickly followed by a loud crack of thunder that caused several women to scream. As soon as the moment passed, there was a round of genial laughter from the crowd.

The orchestra began to play and the sound echoed off the wooden walls and floors, filling the room with music. A few couples stood and moved onto the dance floor.

Looking up from her table at the men talking, Jennie noticed that Newt was almost a full head shorter than Palmer and the others. Judging from his animated gestures, he was explaining some detail about making boxes. It was the only thing that seemed to excite him.

As she watched, she saw Palmer excuse himself and begin across the room towards her table. Despite what she knew about his womanizing and drinking at sordid establishments along the railroad tracks, he still carried an elegant wickedness about him that she couldn't deny she had once found attractive.

"Good evening, Mrs. Rowell," he said. "Would you be so kind as to introduce me to your lovely friend?"

With a strained smile, Jennie said, "Harriet, this is Mr. Palmer, Newt's business partner. Mr. Palmer, this is Mrs. Harriet King, our neighbor."

"Pleased to meet you," said Palmer, extending a hand.

Harriet reached up and gave his hand a quick squeeze. "Likewise, Mr. Palmer."

"Mr. Palmer, I'm sorry to inform you that she's not your type," Jennie said. "Perhaps you would prefer me to introduce you to her husband instead."

"Ah, Jennie, I see you've lost none of your venom since the last time we spoke," Palmer said. Turning to Harriet, he added, "Please forgive me if I have offended you in any way."

"Oh, not at all!" exclaimed Harriet, looking surprised by the tone of the conversation.

"If you will excuse me, then." Palmer nodded at Jennie and walked away towards the bar.

"Jennie! What was all that about?" asked Harriet.

Jennie sighed. "Oh, Harriet, it's such a long story that I wouldn't know where to begin. Let's just say that Mr. Palmer and I have had our differences in the past."

"If you don't mind my asking, with regards to what?"

"He has never forgiven me for stealing Newt away from him. It seems like ever since we married, I have been in competition with Mr. Palmer for Newt's attention. Apparently, he misses his companionship at the brothels."

"How very strange," said Harriet.

"Yes, indeed. Both of them are," replied Jennie, causing Harriet to laugh out loud.

"Oh, Jennie, you are such a wicked girl sometimes!"

"Only sometimes?" said Jennie, smiling.

Outside, the clouds opened, and rain broke against the windows.

CHAPTER ELEVEN

The midsummer sun beat down on the street, shimmering through the canopy of trees. Jennie sat in the shade of the front porch fanning herself against the heat. The laughter and voices of the children playing in the yard mingled with the buzzing of the cicadas. Summer was at its peak.

Newt had left on another trip to Providence a few days before, and now she was alone again with only the girls to keep her company. The days seemed to pass slowly, like the horses pulling wagons down the street. Her thoughts wandered and she didn't notice the girl coming up the street until she turned to walk up onto the front porch.

"Good afternoon, Mrs. Rowell," the young woman said.

Jennie, startled, sat up quickly. "Good afternoon."

"Sorry to disturb you, but Mr. Palmer sent me

round to give this to you," she said, holding out a stack of envelopes. "Seems the mail was delivered to the factory instead."

"Thank you, dear," Jennie replied. "Can I get you something to drink?"

"No, ma'am, I must be getting back or they'll miss me at the shop."

The girl turned to go and Jennie bid her goodbye, then looked down and began sorting through the mail. How odd that the letters would be delivered to the factory. Perhaps they were addressed incorrectly, she thought, but the addresses clearly stated 123 Bank Street. It was then that she noticed Johnson's script. Her heart stopped as she realized that the letter had been opened. She opened it with trembling hands.

Dear Jennie,

Ever since our night together in Rochester, I have not been able to stop thinking about you. I know that it is dangerous for you to try to travel, but I can't help but look forward to seeing you again. Perhaps there is a way I can come to Batavia to see you . . .

Jennie put down the letter and thanked God that Newt was out of town. She gathered the children and took them next door to Harriet's, giving an excuse about needing to run downtown for something, then she set out for the factory.

As she walked, her anger rose. Who was Palmer to be opening her mail? What business was this of his? It was bad enough that he'd inserted himself into their personal lives before, but she would not tolerate him spying on her again.

Her pace quickened and her footsteps pounded the slate sidewalks as she made her way downtown to the box factory. She climbed the stairs to the third floor, opened the door and stepped into the office.

Palmer was at his desk reading when she slammed the door behind her. His mouth stood open as she crossed the room and waved the letter in his face.

"It would be a little more agreeable to me to read my own letters first!" she shouted.

Palmer smiled, which only infuriated her more.

"How dare you open my mail!"

"Why, Jennie, I have no idea what you are talking about," he said.

"Don't lie to me," Jennie said. "I'm not a fool."

"Nor am I," he replied, leaning back in his chair, "but the same cannot be said for your husband. Does he know you are still seeing Lynch?"

"Newt has nothing to do with this. I am a grown woman, and I do not answer to him or any man."

"That may be, but I'm certain he would not be pleased to find out what you are doing while he's away."

"There are many things I can do without him finding out."

Palmer stood and walked to the doorway of the production room and closed the door. Turning, he said, "I don't doubt it. Newt can be a blind fool." Crossing the room towards her and lowering his voice, he asked, "Tell me, Jennie, does he make you happy?"

Jennie looked away out the window, saying, "Newt

is as cold as an iceberg. I deserve to have other company."

"It isn't Newt I'm referring to," said Palmer. "I know that a man like Newt isn't capable of satisfying a woman with your ambitions. I've known it since the day you met. I mean the young lawyer, Mr. Lynch. Does he make you happy?"

Jennie looked back at Palmer. The room was quiet in the oppressive heat. She lifted her handkerchief and dabbed at the sweat on her temple. Outside the windows the only sound was the slap of water in the trough on the street below. Palmer stepped closer.

"Perhaps there are other ways to meet your needs," he said. "Ways that are closer and within your reach."

Jennie stared into his eyes, and she knew. She had seen that look before in the eyes of other men, but in this case it wasn't a look she had been expecting.

"You said it yourself, Jennie, there are many things you can do without Newt finding out," Palmer continued. "Perhaps I could be persuaded to forget what I know."

Jennie opened her mouth to speak, but Palmer grabbed her and pulled her close. He pressed his mouth against hers and she could feel his tongue prying between her lips. He held her tightly in his arms. She turned her head and struggled to push him away.

"Don't look so surprised, Jennie. I'm sure it's not the first time you have been kissed like this."

"Let go of me!" Jennie said through gritted teeth.

Palmer released her and she pulled away.

"Newt will be gone for another week. Perhaps by the time he has returned I'll have forgotten what I read. But that is entirely up to you."

Jennie met his gaze and stared into his dark eyes and she straightened her dress. "I have never had a high opinion of you, Mr. Palmer, and hearing your proposal is enough to make me ill. There are reptiles I find less disgusting."

A smile crossed Palmer's face. "If you change your mind, you'll know where to find me," he said, laughing.

As she left the office, shame and anger burned in her cheeks. The air was so thick it was hard to breathe, and her chest hurt with the effort.

Would he tell Newt what he knew? She held the letter in her hand. Palmer had no proof of anything. She could just as easily tell Newt of his indecent proposal. Who would Newt believe, and did it matter? He was too timid to do anything, even if he knew.

When she got back to the house she took out her stationery and began to write Johnson a letter. She had to see him again. She had nothing more to lose.

CHAPTER TWELVE

Standing in front of the bathroom mirror, Newt's fingers moved with practiced deftness as he tied his bow tie. He wet his comb and pulled it through his thinning hair, working it over in an effort to hide the growing bald spot on the crown of his head. He had never been a man who cared much about his outward appearance. Substance mattered much more than style, which made it all the more strange that he felt self-conscious about his hair. Perhaps he was finally starting to feel his age.

He said goodbye to Jennie and the children and set off for work. The buzz of cicadas was already rising as he walked down the tree-lined street towards Main. It would be another hot late-summer day at the factory. Not the sort of weather that was conducive to good work from the girls in the workshop. If it kept up like this, they would struggle to keep up with orders.

Newt removed his hat as he entered the building and began climbing the stairs to the third floor. His footsteps echoed as his eyes slowly adjusted to the shadowy stairwell. Opening the door to the office and hanging his hat on the rack, he crossed the room towards Palmer's desk.

"Good morning," he said.

"Welcome home, Newt. I was wondering if you came in on the train last night."

"Yes, I got in around six, but went straight home."

"And Jennie and the girls?"

"Fine, fine. Although the girls seem to have grown an inch since I left. How's business?"

"Fair enough. We finished the Boston order yesterday and will be shipping it out this morning."

"Good, good. You'll be happy to know I'm bringing home another order, this one for five thousand pieces. The headache powder is selling better than we thought."

"To be expected, if you have to listen to those New Englanders speak for any length of time," said Palmer, grinning.

The first shift would not arrive until eight o'clock. In the cool morning air, Newt could smell the freshly oiled machines.

"I see you've attended to the lines already," he said. "I'm beginning to think you never sleep."

"Well, someone has to keep this place running while you're out hunting elephants."

Newt smiled, glad to be back after two long weeks

on the road. The humidity of the East Coast in the summertime always seemed to suck the energy out of him. He sat down to look through the stack of mail on his desk.

"I've been thinking of hiring a secretary to look after things once we're done with the expansion," Palmer said. "It will give me more time to tend to the lines."

"Will I have to hire a chaperone to watch over you two while I'm away?" Newt said, winking.

Palmer paused, and a serious look crept across his face.

"I'm not sure how to tell you this, Newt, so I'll just come right out with it. Perhaps it isn't me you should be hiring a chaperone for when you are away."

Newt put the envelopes down and looked up queerly at Palmer. "What are you trying to say?"

"I'm afraid you know all too well what I'm implying."

Newt looked at him in silence.

"Some letters were mistakenly delivered to the office while you were away. In my haste, I opened one without reading the address closely."

Newt looked away out the window at the brick buildings glowing orange in the morning sun.

"It was a letter to Jennie, from her friend the lawyer."

Outside the window, Newt could hear horses whinnying in the street.

"What did it say?" he asked, still looking out the window.

"Just what you would imagine it said," replied

Palmer. "She's been seeing him again."

"How can you be certain? Did he say that in the letter?" Newt turned to meet Palmer's eyes.

"Don't be a fool, Newt."

Newt ran his hand through his hair and leaned forward on his elbows. "I cannot believe it. How can you be certain that they've seen each other?"

"He said as much in the letter."

"Where is it?" Newt asked, his voice rising as he looked up at Palmer.

"When I realized my mistake, I resealed the envelope and had one of the girls deliver it to Jennie."

Newt's head began to ache and he rubbed his temples. "Then I must speak to her at once."

"If she's been seeing that adulterer, do you think she will confess it?" said Palmer. "Listen to me, Newt."

"I must speak to her. I need to hear it from her." Newt stood and crossed the room quickly, leaving without his hat. His footsteps echoed down the steps.

Could it be? Could she really have begun seeing him again? Surely there must be some explanation. It had been over a year since they left Utica. It couldn't possibly be true.

Passing the storefronts and pedestrians as the village came to life, Newt was lost in his thoughts. The shopkeeper at Lorish's Grocery waved at him, but he walked past unseeing.

He looked up to find himself in front of his home. He stood there silently for a minute or two before he climbed the front steps and opened the door.

"Mr. Rowell, what on earth are you doing home?"

Jennie said as he entered the parlor.

The girls ran to him and he absentmindedly patted them on the head.

"We must talk. I've something I need to ask you."

A shadow passed across Jennie's face, and she quickly took the girls by the hands and led them to the kitchen, saying, "Run along and play outside now, girls, while Mummy and Daddy talk."

Returning to the parlor, she asked, "What is it, Newt? You look as though you've seen a ghost."

"Perhaps I have," he replied, looking down at the rug.

"What do you mean?"

"Jennie, have you been seeing Lynch?" he asked, his voice catching.

"Why on earth would you ask me that?" Jennie answered, her own voice rising.

"I need to know it, Jennie. I need to hear it from you."

"Newt, how dare you make such an accusation!"

"Just tell me if you have, Jennie."

"Of course not."

"I . . . I'm . . ." said Newt, pausing.

Jennie was silent, looking at him with flushed cheeks and tears welling in her eyes. Newt looked away.

"I hear things, Jennie, and I don't know what to believe."

She turned away from him and left the room. Standing alone in the sunlit parlor, Newt considered going after her to apologize, but hesitated. After several minutes he turned and left the house.

He wandered for what may have been hours until he found himself alongside the train tracks that bisected the heart of Batavia. Looking east and then west, he saw the shining steel rails disappear in the haze. The clouds hung like wisps of cotton pasted to the sky.

Could he really believe her? He had seen nothing to make him doubt her words, aside from Palmer's insistence. But why should Palmer lie? There were no clear answers.

Kicking the cinders along the edge of the tracks, he could hear the far-off thrumming of an engine in the distance. He felt as helpless as a passenger on that train, hurtling ahead into a future he could not control.

Later, as the sun was working lower into the sky, he returned to the office. Palmer was not at his desk and Newt did not enter the factory floor to look for him. Collecting his hat from the rack, he closed the door behind him and left for the night.

♦

A week passed, and with each passing day Newt found it harder and harder to concentrate on his work. Jennie hardly spoke to him and he could hardly think of anything to say to her to excuse his doubts. He stopped eating lunch, the ache gnawing at his stomach.

Walking the streets he felt as if at any moment he might see the face of Lynch appear ahead of him. He entered his home each evening unsure of whether

Jennie would still be there. He could take it no longer, he decided, and he approached her one night when she was knitting in the parlor.

"Jennie, it was wrong of me to accuse you so. Can you ever forgive me?"

Jennie sat in her chair with the wool yarn stretched across her lap and did not look up at him. The glow of the oil lamp beside her lit up the strands of her blonde hair as if they were threads of gold.

"I don't know what came over me. I heard someone repeat a rumor, and I didn't know what to think. All the memories of what happened in Utica came flooding back and I had a moment of weakness. I never should have doubted you."

Jennie looked up at him. The red and gold hues of the room were glowing in the shadows behind her.

"I have given you everything I have to give, Newt. Two children, a home to comfort you, and all of my friends and family. I'm not sure what more you can ask of me . . ." Her voice trailed off.

"It was wrong of me, dear. It's just that the thought of losing you drove me mad. If you were to leave me, I'm not sure what I would do."

"I have never once said anything about leaving you, Newt. You are the one that insisted on moving the family here from Utica, and I went along, didn't I? Why is it so hard for you to trust me? Must I always live under this shadow of doubt?"

"It was just . . . Palmer told me about the letter he opened by mistake. The situation didn't look right, and I began to doubt you."

"Mr. Palmer needs to mind his own business, and

stop prying into the mail of others!" Jennie shouted. "Am I not allowed to have a private life? Must I live in a glass bowl like a goldfish?"

"No, dear . . ." Newt said, looking down at the rug.

"Then tell your friend Mr. Palmer to leave us alone. Remind him that I am your wife. He is just your business partner."

"Yes, dear, I shall have a talk with him," Newt said meekly.

The flame of the oil lamp began to gutter and light flickered through the room. The pattern on the wallpaper looked for a moment like the scorch marks of flames. Jennie reached over and adjusted the wick.

"I'll be glad when the gas fixtures are installed, so we can do away with these infernal lamps."

"I'll speak to the gas company tomorrow to find out when they'll have the line finished," Newt said. "I imagine they'll want to fill the trench in again before winter."

Jennie nodded and returned to her knitting. Newt stood before her for a moment, then turned and left the room.

◆

The office had grown uncomfortable since their discussion about the letter. Palmer had not raised the topic, and Newt had done his best to devise reasons to stay away from the office. He met with the banker to discuss the expansion and busied himself with accounting. Palmer kept to the shop floor, working on the machines and sketching new designs.

Finally, at the office one afternoon after the girls had gone home for the day, Palmer asked, "Has Jennie said anything more about me opening the letter?"

"Yes." Newt nodded his head. "She was quite upset when we discussed it."

"And did she have an explanation?"

Newt was silent.

"Newt, I understand if you don't believe me. It's my word against hers, and I realize that puts you in a tight spot. I just ask that you do one thing for me, as a friend. Go to the Powers Hotel in Rochester and ask for the registry for the night of August second. There will be registered one Johnson Lynch, and one Mrs. E. N. Potter."

Newt looked at him.

"Please, just do it and you'll see with your own eyes," Palmer said.

Newt nodded, but said nothing.

The next morning Newt left home at his usual time, but instead of going to the office he went to the station and caught the early train to Rochester.

The late summer sun rose on the fields, lighting up the wheat like gold. In the big red barns along the tracks, the farmers were readying for harvest, yoking McCormick reapers and Johnston harvesters to teams of horses to mow the fields, their reels turning like steamship paddles on an ocean of wheat. Newt closed his eyes, but woke with a start when the train came to a halt in the Rochester station. He stepped into the street and hailed a cab for the Powers Hotel.

In the cool dimness of the lobby, Newt screwed up his courage to approach the desk manager. They spoke briefly before the manager went back into the office and returned a moment later with a large register. Placing it upon the marble counter, he opened its leather covers and turned the pages before coming to rest on the one in question. He turned the ledger around and pointed to the entries for August second.

Perspiring greatly, Newt scanned the list, his heart beating faster as his eyes descended row by row. Finally they saw what he had feared. In curious, flowery script was the name of Johnson L. Lynch. There, a few lines below it, was the name Mrs. E. N. Potter, in Jennie's clear handwriting. He felt a stabbing pain in his gut as he thanked the desk manager and turned to leave the hotel, his cheeks flushed with shame and anger.

No matter how hard he tried to put it out of his mind, he kept picturing the two of them secreted in an upstairs room; Jennie reclining in bed, her blonde hair undone and spread across the pillows, a smiling, muscular Lynch on top of her, covering her completely with his bulk as she cried out in pleasure. Newt stopped at the curb and became ill, oblivious to passersby. Wiping his face with a handkerchief, he continued on his way back to the train station.

All the way home, he kept imagining the two of them making love, until finally hot tears began to sting his cheeks. He looked out the window to hide his face. By the time the train stopped in Batavia, he was exhausted. The tears had stopped, but his eyes were swollen and red. The other passengers looked at him curiously as he stood to exit.

It took all his energy to walk back to the office. He kept his head down all the way and did his best to avoid meeting anyone in the street. In the safe, cool darkness of the factory stairwell at last, he climbed the stairs to his office and opened the door.

Palmer frowned when he saw his face. "Well, what did you find?" he asked as Newt sat down heavily.

"Enough, but I don't want to discuss it."

"I told you he was a scoundrel!"

Trying to regain his composure, Newt said between sobs, "I warned her about him. I warned her about him." He tried to draw in a deep breath, but coughed. Hot tears poured from his eyes again; there was no more hope of hiding them. After a few more breaths, he continued with his voice cracking and tears flowing freely down his cheeks. "What more could I have done? I ask you! How could she betray me so?"

Palmer paused in thought. "Newt, in a situation like this you cannot blame the woman. Women are weak-willed and prone to all sorts of ridiculous fancies. A man like Lynch preys upon women. With you out of the way on business, he could shower her with attention and put all manner of thoughts into her head."

Looking thoughtfully at his hands, Newt said, "Since Utica, I have always feared that she was spending her time in the company of another man when I'm gone. She has always been such a vain girl, so eager for attention. Moving her here, where she knew not a soul, was a poor idea. I ought not to have done it. It only made her weaker."

"Perhaps there is a way you can get her back."

"What do you mean?"

Palmer leaned forward in his chair and looked across the desks at Newt. "Perhaps if someone were to teach that scoundrel a lesson, he would learn to stay away from another man's possessions."

Newt wiped his face with his handkerchief, but said nothing.

"If he were to remove himself from the scene, your problems might be solved."

The silence was only broken by the rhythmic clacking of the machines in the other room.

"I'm willing to help you, Newt. Give me some time to think about it."

CHAPTER THIRTEEN

All morning long Newt sat at his desk with an open ledger in front of him, staring out the window at the pigeons roosting on the ledge. Palmer had been busy in the factory, but now he sat in the chair opposite Newt with his coat off and his shirtsleeves rolled up, the blond hair on his muscular forearms glistening with sweat.

"To catch a rat, you need a trap," Palmer said, bringing his open palm down on the table. He leaned forward with an excited look on his face. "The bait is obvious. All we need to do is to find a way to lure him in and spring the trap on him."

Newt looked across at his old friend, unsure of where this was going but too tired to ask questions.

"If we can get him into the house and surprise him, we could teach the bastard a lesson."

"He is a big man," said Newt. "It will take more than one man to subdue him."

"I'm not suggesting that you try to overpower him alone."

Newt looked at him.

"I know a few boys down at the billiard saloon that would be happy to assist. Three or four of us could easily overpower him."

"And what then?"

"I have an idea of a way that we can humiliate the man so he never shows his face again."

"I'm not sure," said Newt. "How can you be certain it will work?"

"Dandies like Lynch are all the same. He plays the gentleman while he looks for weak and vulnerable women. I'm sure Jennie's not the only one he's seduced."

Newt winced.

"Once he's publically revealed as the criminal he is, his career will be ruined. He'll have no choice but to flee and start his life over in some faraway hovel where nobody knows him. Then you need never fear him again."

"And Jennie?"

"All women want to see their man stand up and fight for them. After seeing you drive him out, she will naturally be enamored of you and forget him entirely."

The next night, when they had closed up the office for the day, Newt went with Palmer to Blodgett's saloon. The wind on the street was whipping up dust clouds as the weather began to change. Already a hint of fall was in the air. The billiard tables looked like little fields of green grass as he stepped into the warm gaslit saloon. A big man in the corner sat waiting his turn to shoot while a tall thin man leaned over one of the tables lining up a shot. The cue sent the ball spinning across the green felt, where it clacked into another and rolled into the pocket.

Grinning, Palmer called out, "Harris, you fox, I see you're taking Vallet's money again."

"God forbid I have to rely on this drunkard's wallet to make a living," Harris answered.

Palmer laughed and slapped Vallet on the back, saying, "James, Charles, I'd like to introduce you to my partner, Mr. Rowell."

"Pleased to make your acquaintance, Mr. Rowell," said Harris. "Palmer has told us much about you."

"Please, call me Newt," Newt answered.

Palmer ordered a round of whiskey. The barkeeper nodded and motioned them to a table. It had been over a year, but before Jennie and the girls moved to town Newt had been there frequently. It was one of many hangouts where Palmer drank and spent his money on the companionship of women. Nothing had changed. The same sawdust floors, the same worn chairs and weathered tables. Stepping into Blodgett's was like stepping back to the turn of the century. Newt could picture men in breeches and riding boots drinking tankards of ale.

The discussion moved quickly to the business at hand. Hearing Palmer speak so openly about his situation caused Newt to blush. He hoped it was hidden in the dim light. He could feel Harris and Vallet judging him and he regretted coming. Palmer laid out his plan for trapping Lynch in the act, stripping him, and turning him out into the street. The final coup de grace would be to mail Lynch's clothes to the newspaper in Utica with an account of the incident.

They talked for an hour until Newt stood and said it was time to get home before Jennie became suspicious. Palmer stood and followed him outside. The gaslights shone like moons all up and down Main Street. The streets were nearly empty as they walked back past the factory on their way home. Newt looked ahead into the darkness and could just make out the silhouette of the steeple of First Baptist Church. Turning to Palmer, he said, "I'd like to sell my share of the business."

Palmer stopped walking and looked at Newt with surprise. "What?"

"I'd like to sell my half of the business back to you."

"Why ever do you want to do that?"

Newt continued walking, looking down at the granite sidewalk. "I've been thinking about it these past few weeks. Perhaps if I could just get away for a while and clear my head I could focus on Jennie, and saving our marriage."

"Newt, things will get better once Lynch is taken care of, I'm sure of it."

"I don't know that it will. I can't sleep, I can't eat, and I find it impossible to focus on work. I'm not doing the business any good in this condition."

"Newt, I refuse to accept your offer. Take a week and think it over. I'm sure you'll change your mind." Palmer put his hand on Newt's shoulder.

When they reached the corner of Bank Street, Newt agreed he would think about it, but said he'd already thought a lot about it and had made up his mind. He said goodnight and turned towards home.

♦

Jennie entered the parlor carrying the tea set on a silver tray, with Harriet a few steps behind her holding a plate of cookies. They set everything down on the coffee table and Jennie smiled at Mr. King, who was on the sofa across from Newt. "Would you like milk or sugar, Hiram?" she asked as she poured him a cup of tea.

Newt watched her silently as she poured, the tip of her tongue slightly protruding from the corner of her mouth as she concentrated. Her blonde hair was starting to slip from the pins that held it up behind her ear. He looked at her tiny ears, at the pearl earrings he gave her after a trip to Boston. They glimmered next to the whiteness of her neck, catching the sunlight that flooded the room. Good God, but she was beautiful. He thought about the softness of her skin and the comfort of her scent as she lay next to him in bed at night, and the pain in his stomach only got worse.

"Newt, Jennie tells me you'll be travelling again," Harriet said.

"Oh . . . indeed," Newt said distractedly.

"Whereabout are you headed this time?" asked Hiram.

Newt paused for a moment. "West. I am going out west," he said, then added, "to Washington."

Furrowing his brow, Hiram looked at Newt strangely. "West? I would rather have thought Washington were south of here."

Newt stared at him blankly.

"Oh, I'm sure it gets difficult to keep it all straight, with as many places as you visit," said Harriet, looking at Hiram.

"Yes, Newt does like to keep the railroads in business," Jennie said. "I wish sometimes that he would take me along to see these places."

"Oh, wouldn't that be exciting," said Harriet. "Perhaps someday when the kids are grown you two can get away."

Jennie nodded, offering a faint smile.

The discussion continued on to other things and Newt became lost again in his thoughts. Despite the bright sunshine, the windows were closed against the late October chill. It wouldn't be long before the first hard frost. This was his favorite time of year; the leaves flaming red and orange, the chrysanthemums still holding their blooms. It was like nature was throwing one last celebration before the gray descent of winter. Outside the gas lines had finally been finished and the trenches filled in. Now the workmen would get busy installing light fixtures inside. Perhaps the bright lights of the new lamps would lift his spirits as the nights grew longer and the darkness deepened. Only the laughter of his children had kept him going lately.

Newt excused himself to check on the children.

He climbed the stairs to the girls' room and stood in the doorway watching Clara, Edna, and the Kings' daughter play with the dollhouse. How simple it all seemed. Soon he would win her back. Soon he would take her on the trips she so dearly wanted. Palmer had accepted his offer to sell his half of the business, promising to sell it back at the same price if he changed his mind. Perhaps someday he would change his mind. For now, though, selling the business would give him the time and money he needed to show Jennie he was a better man than Lynch. They would travel; Chicago, Boston, Philadelphia, New York. He would call on his business contacts and secure a position somewhere. They could move into a townhome on a paved street, hire a nanny, turn their lives into the dollhouse Jennie had always wanted.

One week later, he packed his bags and said goodbye to Jennie and the girls. He left for the station as if he would catch a train, but instead checked into a hotel just south of the station, asking for a room on the second floor overlooking the station's front entrance. He set his valise on the dresser, sat on the edge of the bed, and waited.

♦

"I spoke to the telegraph office and told them you're expecting an important telegram from Utica, and to have it delivered to the office at once," Palmer said. "I'm sure we'll know within the day if he's coming."

"And what if he doesn't?"

"Don't worry, Newt. Be patient, he'll come."

"I wish I shared your confidence, but waiting in this hotel is killing me. I spend all day pacing. Every time a train arrives from the east I scan the crowd from my window like some Pinkerton."

Palmer laughed. He put his hand on Newt's shoulder and reassured him the plan would work. "Come for a walk with me, Newt. I have something to give you, and this isn't the place for it." He finished his drink and put some coins on the bar, nodded to the barkeeper and led the way outside.

The morning sun was hidden behind low gray clouds as the men crossed Jackson Street. Newt looked around, feeling like everyone was watching them, aware of what they were doing. On the west side of the street, Palmer turned and followed a rutted path along the railroad tracks toward the creek. Newt walked silently, wondering where Palmer was taking him. The path led past the gasworks and behind several warehouses before emerging onto a grassy field by the bridge over the creek.

"This looks like a good spot," said Palmer as he reached into his coat pocket. Newt's eyes widened as Palmer's hand emerged holding a large pistol.

"You never said anything about a gun."

"Hear me out, Newt. I've been thinking it over, and I've decided it would be best if you had something to hold Lynch in place, should we be delayed."

"You're not suggesting I shoot the man?"

"Not at all. It's merely to scare him, and get him to sit still until we arrive." Palmer handed the gun to Newt.

Newt turned it over in his hand, amazed at the weight of it. The smooth bore barrel shone, even in the overcast. "I've never used a gun before in my life."

"Here, I'll show you how to use it," said Palmer, taking the gun back. He lifted it and aimed at a tree on the opposite bank of the creek, and demonstrated how to fire it. "Now, try it," he said, handing it back.

Newt lifted the gun and pointed at the same tree. His hand shook as he pulled the trigger and the gun discharged. The gunshot echoed off the buildings and startled him. He was amazed, not by the power of the gun, but by how easy it was to fire it. The simplicity of the movement belied its power.

"See, you've got it."

"I don't intend to use it," Newt said, as much to himself as to Palmer.

"Still, keep it on your person. He's a large man, and there's no telling what he might do when he's caught. An animal is most dangerous when cornered."

Newt looked at the revolver in his hand and was suddenly self-conscious that someone would see them with it. He quickly hid it inside his coat, feeling the heat of the barrel warm his pocket.

"Come, let's get back before anyone comes looking for me. You should stay out of sight until the moment arrives."

Newt nodded and followed Palmer through the field as a slow freight train came steaming past, pulling out of the siding and onto the main line. Black smoke poured from the stack and hung low in the heavy sky, the soot sifting slowly down like black snow onto the warehouses.

CHAPTER FOURTEEN

The sun was setting behind the cupola on the old courthouse as Newt stepped out of the hotel into the street. He hurried across the tracks and headed west on Ellicott Street, trying not to run as his heart raced inside his chest. He looked up at the courthouse's limestone walls glowing pink in the setting sun. He scanned the street for familiar faces, but the streets were empty save for a few passengers heading toward Ellicott House.

What would it matter if he was seen by his neighbors? They'd assume he was hurrying home for dinner. Little would they know that it was Johnson Lynch that his wife was waiting for in the front parlor. It was Lynch she was thinking of as she put on perfume and her finest dress. It was Lynch who was on a train at that very moment, probably carrying a note from Jennie in his hands. Newt's heart burned with shame and tears welled up in his eyes.

The gun weighed heavy in his coat pocket. He felt along the cool steel barrel with his sweaty hand, over the chamber and down along the ivory handle. In his other pocket, he felt the bag filled with black pepper. How long would it be before Palmer arrived with Harris and Vallet? Two hours at the most? Could he keep quiet in his house for that long, knowing that Lynch was eating at his table, sitting in his own chair in the parlor? Or would the pain become so great that he wouldn't be able to keep from crying out? His vision blurred as he crossed Main and walked up State Street.

If he hurried, Newt was sure he could get home and inside before the train arrived. He was almost at a run now, his feet slapping hard against the bluestone slate sidewalk, sending shivers through the bones of his legs. Turning in at Hutchins Place, he walked until he came to the house behind his own, then slipped through the long cool shadows of the maple trees in his back garden, past the rose bushes Jennie planted that spring, barren now except for the brown leaves curled on the vines. The girls would be playing in the nursery or next door with the Kings. Yes, he thought, Jennie would have asked Harriet to watch the children for the night. She wouldn't invite a lover into the house while the children were there. She was impetuous and impulsive, but not that foolish.

He climbed the back steps and stood panting at the door. He waited for a few moments to quiet himself, and then gently turned the knob and pushed the door open. The kitchen was empty. He stepped slowly towards the back stairs, listening for voices and taking great care to place his feet on the edges of the steps, where they were least likely to squeak. He felt like a child playing hide and seek with Palmer at his father's house, only now the gun was real.

Oh, why had he agreed to take the gun? He hardly knew how to use the thing. Surely there would be no need for it. He would surprise them and rub the pepper in Lynch's eyes. Then when he was writhing on the floor he could use anything to overpower him. He knew Lynch was a big man, almost a full foot taller than Newt, but lying in bed blinded by pepper, the fight would be equal.

Yes, he would just keep the gun in his pocket in case something went wrong. He would find another way to subdue him.

Newt paused on the stairs and considered his options. A skillet would be too unwieldy, a rod from the fireplace too likely to hit Jennie. Turning, he started back down the stairs and slipped out the kitchen door.

The sunlight was gone and dusk was descending quickly. He searched through the garden beds until he found a smooth stone the size of a child's fist. He put it in his pocket and started back into the house. As he opened the door, he heard voices coming down the hallway. He froze.

"Jennie, do you really want me to stay with you?" It was Harriet King.

"Oh, Harriet, please," he heard Jennie say. "I know it sounds silly, but I'm afraid to see him again.

The thought of him being on his way here is making me giddy. Please stay for a few minutes until I calm down."

"Very well, then, I'll stay, but only for tea. Then I'll leave you two alone and go back to the children. The housekeeper leaves at seven and Hiram will be cross if I stay any longer."

Newt's face flushed with embarrassment. How could she be so brazen as to invite the neighbor in to meet her lover? Had she no sense of shame? Hearing her speak glowingly of Lynch stabbed him with pain. He held his breath and stepped quickly into the stairway and began to climb again before they got to the kitchen to prepare tea.

The upstairs was dark in the gloaming. Newt stepped lightly down the hallway and entered Jennie's sewing room. He was sure to be able to hear everything in the parlor, and Jennie would have no need to enter this room. He stood quietly by the doorway, listening to the women in the kitchen. He turned the cold stone over and over in his pocket, thinking about how round and smooth it was, like an egg.

He tried to picture how he would surprise them in the dark and rub black pepper in Lynch's eyes. He imagined Lynch howling with pain and thrashing on the bed as he raised the rock to smash him.

If Lynch came to, Newt would use the gun to hold him until Palmer and the men arrived. Then they would strip him and send him out naked into the streets to humiliate him and teach him a lesson. Now there was only waiting.

In a few moments, Newt heard footsteps on the front porch, then the ringing of the bell.

CHAPTER FIFTEEN

Jennie ran to the front door and looked through the glass panes at Johnson Lynch's tall silhouette on the porch. She opened the door and welcomed him in.

"Well, Mr. Lynch, I see you've come bearing gifts."

He presented a bouquet of lilies and removed his hat. "For you, my dear, though they are but the merest reflection of your beauty."

Jennie laughed, taking the flowers and leaning forward to give him a kiss on his cheek.

"Please come in and allow me to introduce you," she said as she took his coat. "There's someone I would like you to meet."

Raising his eyebrows in surprise, Johnson followed her into the parlor.

"Mrs. King, please allow me to introduce my dear friend Johnson Lynch. Mr. Lynch, this is Mrs. Harriet King, my closest friend and neighbor."

"Pleased to meet you, Mrs. King," Johnson said, bowing low and taking her hand.

Blushing, Harriet said, "Please, the pleasure is mine. I've heard so much about you, Mr. Lynch."

"Lies, I am sure," Johnson replied. "I am not half the scoundrel Jennie has made me out to be."

"Oh, quite the contrary," Jennie said. "You are at least twice as dangerous as I've told her."

Turning to Harriet, she cautioned, "Be on your guard around this man, Harriet. He has been known to ruin the reputation of many a good woman."

"You sound as if you speak from experience," he said.

"You should be so fortunate," Jennie replied, and Harriet laughed with embarrassment.

Placing the flowers in a vase on the mantle, Jennie invited them to sit down while she brought the tea.

"Mrs. King, Jennie has told me what a dear friend you've become since she moved to Batavia."

"Please, call me Harriet. Jennie has told me much about you as well."

"Yes, we've known each other for quite a while," Johnson said. "We miss her in Utica. It hasn't been the same since she moved away."

"I'm sure of it," Harriet replied. "I must say that I'm the one who has benefited most by her move. Life here was dreadfully boring before Jennie came to town."

Jennie returned to the parlor carrying a tea tray and

a plate of oysters. "Oh, dear, what has he been telling you?"

"I was just telling Harriet that our loss has been her gain," said Johnson.

"And I was agreeing," Harriet said, smiling.

The light outside was fading as Jennie lit the oil lamp on the table. She shivered in the chill of the late autumn air.

"Are you warm enough, dear?" Jennie asked. "Would you like me to start a fire to take the chill out?"

"No, I'm quite comfortable," Harriet said, not realizing that she had been speaking to Johnson. In the lamplight, Johnson's features seemed even more pronounced. The curve of his mustache, the waves of his hair, he seemed ten years younger than the last time she saw him. He seemed to sense her eyes upon him, and smiled, returning her gaze.

"Please excuse my manners," Johnson said as he helped himself to the oysters. "I'm ravenous."

"By all means," Harriet said, but Jennie hardly heard her.

She sat down next to Johnson, asking, "How was the trip?" when the bell rang. She rose to greet Hiram King at the door.

"I beg your pardon, Jennie, but I'm coming to get Harriet," he apologized.

"Please, won't you come inside?" Jennie said, stepping back from the door.

"No, thank you, I just came to get Harriet. She's needed at home."

Harriet came into the foyer. "Is everything all

right?"

"Aside from the children waiting to see you and the housekeeper wanting to go home, yes, everything is fine."

Harriet glared at him.

"I'm sorry, it's my fault," Jennie interrupted. "An old friend of mine from Utica has dropped in to visit, and I insisted on introducing him to Harriet. Please, why don't you come inside and join us for dinner? I'm sure we could call the Showerman girl and have her stay with the kids while we visit. I have a deck of cards, and we need a foursome anyway for bridge."

"Yes, please come inside," Harriet repeated.

"No, really. We must be getting home," Hiram said, meeting his wife's gaze.

Harriet turned back into the parlor and said, "I'm sorry, Mr. Lynch, but I have to run. It was a pleasure meeting you."

"Yes, it was a pleasure to meet you," Johnson replied, standing now and making a slight bow. "I hope we see you again soon."

"Goodnight, Jennie," Harriet said. "I apologize for our rudeness."

"Oh, dear, there's no need for apologies. I understand." Jennie reached out to squeeze Harriet's hand, then closed the door and returned to the parlor.

"Is everything all right?" Johnson asked.

"Yes," Jennie responded, "although I'm afraid I've gotten poor Harriet into a bit of trouble."

"Hmm ... I see nothing has changed," Johnson said. "You still have your talent for stirring up trouble."

Jennie laughed as she crossed the room to him. "Now for a real kiss," she said, putting her arms around his shoulders.

Johnson lowered his head to meet her mouth and she tasted the salt from the oysters on his lips. She held that kiss for a long moment, letting go of all the worry and tension that had built as she waited for him to arrive.

"I suppose I promised you dinner," she said. "Perhaps I should get busy in the kitchen."

Johnson smiled. "Jennie, you are the only nourishment I need."

She went to the windows and closed the shades against the darkness outside. The glow of the lamp's frosted globe lit the room in a warm yellow light.

Johnson came up behind her as she drew the last of the drapes and put his arms around her, cupping her breasts in his hands and bending down to kiss her neck. Her eyes closed as she surrendered to his touch. She turned to meet his lips with hers. He lifted her gently and carried her to the sofa. She put her arms around his neck and felt the brush of his mustache against her face as he kissed her. She ran her fingers through his hair.

"Oh, how I've longed for you." She sighed as his kisses worked down along her neck to the collar of her dress. He ran his hands up the curve of her waist and pressed them against her breasts. She lifted his head and kissed him, taking his tongue into her mouth. His hands worked to undo the clasps of her dress and she whispered in his ear, "Let's go upstairs."

Thomas Gahr

She took his hand and led him up the steps to the bedroom, where she removed her dress and turned to him. He untied her corset as her hands moved from button to button down the front of his shirt. As her corset fell from her body, she felt his fingers slowly working up her spine like the keys of a piano.

CHAPTER SIXTEEN

Newt stood in the dark across the hallway. He had heard the footsteps on the stairs and he dared not breathe. Now he could hear them breathing and the rustle of their clothes. It seemed as if the sounds were amplified in the darkness. He heard the bedsprings squeak as they lay down and his hand squeezed harder on the gun in his pocket until it seemed to burn against his flesh. With his free hand he reached for the bag of black pepper.

As he stepped quietly across the hallway and into the bedroom, his head ached and his eyes strained to make out their forms. He reached out into the darkness with a handful of black pepper and his fingers felt someone's soft flesh.

Jennie screamed.

Newt fumbled madly with the pepper, swinging his arms wildly, trying to find Lynch's face. Lynch jumped from the bed and leaned his shoulder into Newt, sending him flying backward against the wall. The gun went off and lit the room with a flash like lightning.

Wood splinters flew through the air and rained down on the bed as Jennie kept screaming and Lynch pushed past Newt towards the stairs. Newt followed and raised the gun again, shooting at the silhouette in the stairwell.

One shot rang out, and then another, and Lynch tumbled to the bottom of the stairs and landed with a dull thud, and then all was silent.

Newt could only make out a dark lump in the foyer. Jennie pushed past him and ran down to Lynch's body, crying, "Johnson!"

Newt descended the steps as Jennie ran her hands along Lynch's body and felt his head twisted awkwardly to the side. She ran her fingers though his hair and they came away wet. "No . . . no, no!"

"I had no choice," Newt mumbled. "I had no choice."

"Johnson! Johnson!" she screamed again, but his body lay still beneath her hands. She struggled to turn him and lift him into her arms as Newt descended the steps and walked outside.

"Come quick! I shot a man," he yelled from the porch steps to the voices in the distance. He turned back into the front hallway, stepped over the widening pool of blood, and lit the oil lamp on the table. Jennie sat on the floor beside her lover's body, half naked and crying. She looked up at her husband and screamed again. "Why?!"

Newt turned down the hall to the kitchen, where he filled a bowl with water. When he came back into the entryway Jennie was gone and a neighbor, Mr. Swanson, was kneeling beside the body. Setting down the bowl of water, Newt said, "I found this man seducing my wife and I shot him." Swanson looked up at Newt, his eyes wide with shock.

Taking a rag, Newt bent down and began to wipe Lynch's face. Swanson reached out and stopped him. "Is he dead, then?" asked Newt.

Swanson nodded.

"I was afraid of it," Newt said, and then repeated, "I found him seducing my wife and I shot him."

Another neighbor, John Reed, came through the front door and looked down at Swanson, who gestured at Newt to point out that the gun was still in his hand. Reed put his arm around Newt and calmly said, "Here, Newt, why don't you let me hold that for you?"

"Yes, yes . . ." Newt muttered, sitting down on the steps.

Reed turned to Swanson. "Run next door to the Kings and have them send for the sheriff."

Newt sat quietly on the steps, his head in his hands.

"Tell me again what happened?" Reed asked.

Newt pointed at the lifeless body on the floor in front of him. "I came home and found this man seducing my wife and I shot him."

"Where is Jennie now?" asked Reed.

Newt looked up at him as if he didn't understand.

"Is she all right?"

Nodding silently, Newt turned and pointed up the stairs. "They were in the bedroom. I found them there, and then I shot him as he fled. I didn't mean to kill him."

Reed nodded. "Just sit still and try to relax. We can sort things out when the sheriff arrives."

Jennie stepped out of the bedroom wrapped in her robe, her eyes swollen and red. "How could you?" she screamed at Newt. "You murdered him! You'll hang for this."

Newt nodded and quietly said, "I suppose I shall."

Jennie came halfway down the stairs, then turned and walked quickly back to the top. Running her fingers through her hair, she said, "Why? Why did you shoot him? Why couldn't you just beat him with your fists like any other man would?"

Newt just stared at her.

"You've brought shame and humiliation upon us. We'll never be able to show our faces again."

"I warned her against him," Newt said, looking at Reed. "I warned her." He lowered his head into his hands and said it again. "I warned her . . ."

He looked at Lynch's body at his feet. One arm was underneath it and the other was bent awkwardly to the side, and the head was twisted at an angle in a pool of darkening blood. Newt looked up at the crowd that had gathered on his porch to peer openmouthed at the lifeless body on the floor.

Newt let Reed lead him into the parlor to wait for the police. When Sheriff Southworth arrived, he asked, "Mr. Rowell, are you all right?"

Newt nodded. "I found a man seducing my wife

and I shot him." He said it again, as if repetition would make it seem less unreal.

"Where's the gun?" asked the sheriff.

"Here," said Reed, removing it from his pocket and holding it out to the sheriff. "I took it from him when I found him."

"Was there anyone else here at the time, Mr. Rowell?"

"No," Newt answered. "Just my wife."

"The children?"

"They're at the neighbors'," said Reed.

The sheriff put the gun in his coat pocket and thanked Reed. "If you don't mind, I'll need to ask Mr. Rowell some questions."

Newt did his best to answer the questions the sheriff asked, but in his mind he kept going back to the one indisputable fact that seemed so unreal: he had shot a man. Somehow, in the rush of fear and anger that surged through his body, he had aimed the gun and killed Lynch. It did not seem possible.

The sheriff called out to one of the constables. "See about covering up the windows here. It's time to put an end to the show."

"The coroner should be here soon," Southworth continued. "Mr. Rowell, I'll have the constable take you down to the station." He turned to Robson and said, "Take him out the back door and slip through the yard. No sense giving them any more show than they've already had."

"Would you please come with me, Mr. Rowell?" the constable said, reaching out to put handcuffs on Newt's wrists.

"May I say goodbye to my wife before we leave?"

The constable nodded and led him upstairs to the bedroom. Jennie sat on the edge of the bed holding Lynch's vest to her face, crying. Newt looked around the room and saw a ball from the revolver on the floor and chipped pieces of plaster and brick where it struck the chimney. The wooden headboard was splintered, but there was no blood on the sheets. Jennie looked up at him. "How could you?"

"I warned you, dear."

"Why did you have to kill him? You realize you'll hang for this?"

Newt sighed. "Yes, I suppose I shall."

Jennie's eyes were red, her blonde hair down around her shoulders. Even in this state, Newt thought of how beautiful she was.

"I must be going now," he said, then bent to kiss her, but she turned her head away.

"Won't you kiss me, Jennie?"

She refused to look at him. Shaking his head, Newt turned and left the room. Robson led him down the back stairs to the kitchen to avoid the crowd at the front door.

They stepped outside into the cool dark and as he walked past the lilac bushes, Newt could see the silhouette of the garden bench. He tried to picture himself sitting there on a bright summer day as Jennie trimmed her roses. He thought about how lovely she would look in her sundress and hat as she worked, unaware of him watching her. He got a lump in his throat and thought, "Those days are gone forever now."

They crossed the back yard and passed the house behind his. Stepping out into the street, they turned toward the courthouse and the police station. On Jefferson Avenue, Newt saw three figures approaching. Even from a distance, he could make out Palmer, Harris, and Vallet in the darkness.

Coming closer to them now, he saw them stop in recognition. "Newt, what happened?" Palmer asked.

"I shot the man," Newt said.

"But I don't understand . . ."

"I shot him dead."

Palmer and his friends stood dumbfounded as Newt and the constable continued on their way.

CHAPTER SEVENTEEN

The morning sun was shining across the wall opposite him as Newt opened his eyes. For a moment he was unaware of where he was, then the events of the previous evening came flooding back to him. He sat up in his bunk and looked out through the bars of the jail cell to see Sheriff Southworth reading at his desk.

"Good morning, Mr. Rowell," Southworth said. "I hope you slept well."

Newt nodded, then looked about the cell, empty except for a bed, a small washstand and mirror, and a chamber pot.

"It seems you're famous this morning," said the sheriff, putting down the newspaper. "You've had quite a few callers seeking interviews. I even heard a reporter from the New York Times is due in town tonight."

Newt tried to make sense of what he was saying as the fog slowly lifted from his mind.

"It isn't every day we have such excitement in our sleepy little village," said Southworth, smiling. Newt nodded.

"Let me fetch you some water to clean up with. I expect you'll be having visitors later today. I'll call next door and have Mrs. Southworth fix you some coffee and a little something to eat."

Newt thanked him and looked around the cell as the sheriff left the room. It still did not seem real. He thought, "And yet here I am, a prisoner in a cell. Who would have ever thought me capable of murder?" He felt strange, remorseful, yet somehow oddly exhilarated.

When Southworth returned with water, Newt did his best to make himself presentable. He felt as if he were in a hotel room preparing for a business meeting. Only his stubble gave the hint of something out of place.

Around noon his brother arrived from Utica. It felt good to see a friendly face, but the shock seemed to take a bigger toll on his brother than it did on Newt.

"My God, Newt. What were you thinking?"

"That's the funny part, George. I don't believe I was thinking at all. It just happened."

"Who was the man?"

"It was Lynch. The same one Jennie was seeing back in Utica."

George shook his head.

"I didn't intend for it to happen. I'd hoped to

teach the man a lesson and shame him into leaving her alone. I don't know how it happened, but there was a struggle, and . . . I shot him."

Newt paused, letting the words slowly register. He had shot him. The first shot in the dark bedroom had been out of panic, but he did not stop. He'd followed Lynch into the hall, raised the gun, and fired again as he fled down the stairs. Once, twice? He couldn't remember how many times he pulled the trigger. He just recalled the flash of the gun lighting up the hallway and the sickening sound of the body as it tumbled down the stairs.

"Well, not to worry, Newt. We'll get you out of here. Father spoke with Judge Sutton and he'll be here tomorrow to see to your defense."

"What's to defend? I shot the man dead. The only thing yet to be determined now is if I shall hang."

"Nonsense. There isn't a jury in the country that would hold it against you to shoot a man you found in bed with your wife."

Perhaps he's right, Newt thought. Perhaps there's still hope. Yet what good will that do? My wife and family have been disgraced, my reputation ruined. What is left for me of that life? I could pack a trunk and head west, maybe to California where no one would know me, but what would that accomplish? A life in exile is almost as bad as a life inside the prison of opinion.

When he thought about the girls, his heart began to ache. They didn't deserve this. If anyone was a victim, it wasn't Lynch, Jennie, or himself; it was the girls. They didn't deserve the notoriety that would follow them around like a cloud, the hushed whispers when they entered a room, the taunts of other children when no adults were around to hear. He knew what it was to be an outsider as a child. To be the one singled out for humiliation. Without Palmer, he'd have grown up alone in the world.

Palmer. What had become of Palmer? He'd seen him on his way to jail, but had heard nothing from him since. If only Palmer and the others had come sooner, perhaps they would have subdued Lynch and turned him naked into the streets. Instead the man lay dead in a morgue, his blood forever staining the floor of his front hall.

When George left to see the girls, Newt lay down on the cot and fell back to sleep.

CHAPTER EIGHTEEN

The rain fell against the windowpane as Jennie stared out the window of her bedroom in her parents' home. The November skies were leaden, and poured their rain down upon the furrowed fields surrounding the house. It had been two weeks since that terrible night, and each day passed in a fog of laudanum. Alone at home with only her mother for comfort, she had taken to long periods of solitude, reading and re-reading her letters from Johnson.

She had left town shortly after the murder. Her children were staying with Newt's sister Julia in Utica. She could not bear the thought of spending another night in the house where Johnson had died. Even now, she still woke to the memory of his body lying in a pool of blood. As she lay in bed shaking with fear, sleep was elusive. If not for the medicine, she wouldn't have slept at all. So the nights passed as slowly as the days as she sat in the window, staring out at the world beyond. If not for her mother looking after her, she wouldn't have even brought herself to eat.

As the weeks passed, her mother pressed her to bring the girls to stay on the farm, but Jennie refused. She did not want to see them like this. In her medicine-induced haze, it wasn't their reaction she feared, but her own. There was no way she could explain her fear that she might look upon them and feel nothing. Her mother would never understand that.

She could feel the effects of the laudanum again, a numbness that began in her toes and slowly moved up her body. The coldness moved through her legs and now rose slowly to her breasts. She looked out at the raindrops streaming down the panes. One by one each drop would melt into another until they became one long streak, giving in to gravity and racing downward, ever downward. She leaned her forehead against the cool glass, closed her eyes, and let the fog consume her.

CHAPTER NINETEEN

When the initial hearings were over and the trial date was set for January, Newt's life began to settle into a routine. If it wasn't exactly pleasant in prison, it was far from uncomfortable. He had a cell entirely to himself and the sheriff had allowed him to have a sofa and a small desk brought from home, which came in handy for meetings with his attorneys.

The days grew shorter and he spent long nights reading on the sofa beneath the light of an oil lamp. The sheriff's wife brought his meals, and he was surprised at the number of visitors he received during the daytime. Not just his family, but reporters looking for a story, the pastor from the Baptist church, business acquaintances he had made; people who would never have sought him out before. How odd that killing a man could turn him into a celebrity. He felt at times like a curiosity in a carnival freak show.

The person whose absence was most conspicuous was Palmer. He had visited only once, and then just for a few minutes, to pay Newt back for his share in the company and speak briefly about the factory. With Newt gone he had hired an office manager and was traveling more frequently. He made no mention of Lynch or his complicity in the plan.

Newt wondered if Palmer had chosen to distance himself from him for business reasons. Surely Palmer felt some responsibility. Regardless, he wished Palmer would come by, if for no other reason than to update him on the business.

As Christmas approached, his sister Julia brought the girls in to see him. He had worried about how they would react to seeing him in jail, but the sheriff welcomed him into his home for the afternoon and let Newt entertain them in the parlor. It was wonderful to see their faces and hear their voices again. His greatest fear was forgetting them. At seven and six, they couldn't possibly understand the situation, but like all children they quickly came to accept their new reality.

If only we could be so resilient, Newt thought, our lives would be much simpler. He had written to Jennie weeks earlier, but she had yet to respond. He began to wonder if she would ever speak to him again. Perhaps he had underestimated her feelings for that man. The thought only served to rub salt into the wounds left by her infidelity.

The murder had been the talk of the village for months, and the rumors that swirled around town amazed him. Newspapers from across the state had covered the case closely, and many had sent reporters to interview him despite his refusal to answer their questions. His brother George had taken to clipping the stories for him. It was strange to read about himself in the paper. The Rowell of the broadsheets seemed like a character in a book.

He asked after Jennie whenever he could, but heard nothing.

CHAPTER TWENTY

At ten minutes before seven o'clock on the evening of January nineteenth, Newt stepped out the door of the county jail for the first time since the night of the murder. Arrangements had been made with the district attorney, and with the support of the president of the Genesee County National Bank, his brother George had posted his $3,000 bail. Taking a deep breath of clear, cold night air, Newt smiled as George clapped him on the back.

"How does it feel to be a free man?"

Newt paused a moment. "Let's wait until I'm truly acquitted."

"All in good time, Newt. All in good time," said George. "Come, let's get going. The housekeeper will have dinner waiting."

They stepped quickly out into the frozen ruts of

the empty street and set off for home. The windows along Bank Street shone like gold in the inky blue dark of the winter night. It seemed surreal to be coming home to the house he built for Jennie and the girls. Stepping up onto the front porch and opening the door, he immediately looked to the floor of the landing for a sign of that fateful night. But the wood floor shone back, as polished as it had always been, and any marks on the stairway walls had been cleaned and painted over. The newel post remained half-drilled for the gas fixtures that had yet to be installed, and there was not a trace of blood to be found.

The oil lamps blazed in the parlor as they hung their coats on the rack and went to the dining room. George went to find the housekeeper and Newt sat down at the table, looking around and recalling each fixture and piece of furniture in the house, mentally accounting for the life he'd built there. Wherever he looked, he could see Jennie's hand. From the wallpaper to the vase on the sideboard, she had selected everything. He half imagined it would be her that came in from the kitchen carrying his supper.

George returned from the kitchen and took a seat across from him, then began to fill Newt in on the details of the coming days. They would be meeting the train from Utica in the morning to pick up their sister Julia and the girls, along with their parents and an uncle. They would have a day to visit before the trial.

That night, as he lay in the very same bed where he'd found Jennie and Lynch, Newt recounted the events over and over again in his mind, as if repetition would somehow dull their sharpness. Sometime after midnight, he drifted off to sleep and slept the fitful sleep of an infant.

♦

Jury selection was due to begin Monday morning, and despite the bitter cold a crowd had already gathered on the iron steps of the courthouse by the time the doors opened at nine. Judge Haight had missed his train out of Buffalo and did not arrive until after ten o'clock, but the mood inside the hall was almost festive as the crowd sat and waited. Newt arrived with his brother George, his parents, his sister Julia and the children. The prosecuting attorneys, Safford North and Lucius Bangs, entered shortly afterward, and once the judge had taken his place the crier opened the court.

Turning to the prosecution, Judge Haight asked, "Has the district attorney any work for this court?"

"If the court please, I move the trial of Edward Newton Rowell, indicted for manslaughter for killing Johnson L. Lynch," responded the district attorney.

Turning to the defense team, the judge said, "Mr. Watson, are you ready for the trial of Mr. Rowell?"

"Yes, Your Honor, if the witnesses that have been subpoenaed are in attendance, and I presume they are."

The day passed slowly, but the standing room crowd in the courthouse never seemed to tire of the proceedings. Shortly before lunch, Julia left with the children. Two tables had been set up for the newspaper men, who scribbled notes during the interviews. Newt's mind wandered as the attorneys took turns interviewing jurors, and as the day wore on he leaned his head on the table and fell asleep.

Waking with a start, his face flushed and he looked about the room, but no one seemed to be paying him any attention. The sky outside had begun to fade, and still the interviews continued. By the time the court adjourned for the day only half of the jury was selected.

Putting on his overcoat, Newt exited the hall into a throng of well-wishers. People he had never met were waiting in the hallway to shake his hand and offer encouragement. Surprised and dumbfounded, Newt took their hands and nodded thanks. With his brother George leading the way, he slowly made his way through the crowd and out of the courthouse into the night.

A light snow had begun falling and the gas lamps along Main Street were glowing golden orbs. Wagons bumped over the frozen ruts in the street and the breath of the horses steamed from their nostrils. Walking home, Newt could feel everyone's eyes on him. Six months ago, no one would have recognized him, and now total strangers wished him luck as he passed them on the sidewalk. It was disconcerting to be the center of attention.

His family was waiting for him at home, and as he took off his coat and hung up his hat, the warmth seeped into his bones and took the chill out of his numb cheeks. It was comforting to have his parents, siblings, and children together after being alone for two months. It struck him as funny, but having them all gathered around the dinner table felt almost like a holiday. The only thing missing was Jennie.

He'd read in the newspaper that she was arriving in town that day, having been subpoenaed by the district attorney as a potential witness. She'd made no contact with his family except to send a note to Julia asking her to bring the girls to visit her at the hotel. It was probably for the best, Newt thought, given all the drama of the trial. Meeting her now, in the midst of all that was going on, would only scramble his thoughts further. Still, he found himself secretly hoping she would come to the courthouse just to find out if the feelings she had for him were still there.

CHAPTER TWENTY-ONE

District Attorney Safford E. North rose from his chair, and turning toward the jury, opened the case for the *People vs. E. N. Rowell* and spoke in a calm and conversational voice.

"Gentlemen of the jury, we are here today to hear the case charge of manslaughter against Mr. Edward Newton Rowell for the killing of Johnson L. Lynch on the night of October thirtieth, 1883."

North continued. "Friends, the killing of a person is not something that happens often in a village of this size. It is not something we take lightly or show indifference toward. A tragedy of this sort consumes us, and causes us to ask many hard questions of ourselves and of our neighbors, of what it means to live in a free community where the rule of law and the love of God guide our very consciences. Whatever you may have heard about the victim and the accused, I ask you now to put aside. I am not here to tell you of the guilt or innocence of the accused, but to outline the circumstances of the tragedy that occurred that October night, and to allow you to hear from your fellow citizens as they present the facts of what occurred that night.

"Once you have heard their statements in their own words, I believe you will agree with the case of the prosecution, that Mr. Rowell went to his house on the evening of the shooting for the purpose of carrying out a plan which had been arranged by himself and his former partner in the paper-box-making business, William T. Palmer, to secure evidence against his wife to be used by Rowell in a suit for divorce which he intended to institute, knowing for some time previously that his wife was unfaithful."

"I shall show," said the district attorney, "that the defendant went into his house early in the evening and remained there fully an hour and a half with Mr. Lynch under his roof. Yet he waited until Mr. Lynch and Mrs. Rowell had retired to her private apartments before he noiselessly entered and felt about the bed to learn their positions, at which time he fired the gun he had brought with him for this very purpose, and the horrible tragedy resulted."

A small murmur ran through the crowd as he concluded his opening remarks and called his first witness. Newt sat at the table alongside Judge Sutton and Mr. Watson and listened to the testimony of David E. Mix, a local surveyor and engineer who provided maps and diagrams of the Rowell residence. The district attorney moved to introduce the drawings as evidence as he began to slowly build his case.

The crowd sat in fixed attention as District Attorney North called his next witness, Eugene Swanson, one of the neighbors who was among the first to arrive at the scene of the crime.

"Mr. Swanson," said North, "could you please recount for the court what you heard and saw on the evening of the alleged murder?"

Swanson told the court that he had been sitting in his parlor two doors down from the Rowell house when he heard two pistol shots, one five or six seconds after the other, followed by two more quick shots in succession.

"What did you hear after the sound of the gunshots, Mr. Swanson?" asked the district attorney.

"I heard the rattling sound of a front door, as if someone were trying to open it."

"What did you do at that point?"

"I stepped out onto my porch and saw Mr. Rowell standing on his porch, crying for help."

"And did you speak with Mr. Rowell?"

"I shouted to him to find out what the trouble was, and Mr. Rowell answered, 'Come quick, I've shot a man.'"

"What did you do at that point, Mr. Swanson?"

"I ran back inside to put on shoes and a coat, then I ran to the Rowell house. On my way I met our neighbor, Mr. Reed, and the two of us proceeded to Rowell's."

Swanson recounted what he saw as he entered the

house and found the body of Lynch at the bottom of the stairs, using the drawings provided by the district attorney to explain the position of the body.

"What did you do at that point?"

'That's when I left to get Dr. Morse and the coroner."

"Thank you, Mr. Swanson, that is all I have to ask of you."

The next person sworn in was the neighbor, Mr. Reed. The district attorney asked him to give his version of the events described by Mr. Swanson. When his questioning was complete, Mr. Watson rose for the defense and cross-examined the witness, asking for more details about what he saw that night and about the behavior and demeanor of Newt Rowell.

"Mr. Reed, how long had you lived next to Mr. Rowell?"

"A little over a year."

"In that time, did you have occasion to talk with Mr. Rowell and observe him with his family?"

"Yes, sir, on several different occasions."

"Would you say that Mr. Rowell is a man who was devoted to his family and loved his home, so far as appearances indicated?" asked Watson.

Raising his hand to the judge, the district attorney said, "Your Honor, I object to the question being asked by the defense, on the grounds that the question is not relevant to the events of the evening of the tragedy."

Newt looked around the room as the discussion continued between the judge and the attorneys. There was no sign of Jennie in the crowd, but he could see his family among the strangers, who were listening to the proceedings as if it were theater. He felt his blood begin to rise in his cheeks. It was one thing to read the rumors and gossip in the newspapers, but it was another thing entirely to have to sit and listen without being able to speak a word in his own defense.

The parade of witnesses continued. The district attorney called upon Dr. Morse, followed by Sheriff Southworth and Officer Robson, asking them all to recount what happened on the evening of the murder. Newt felt as if each telling was different from his own memories, yet not in any way significant enough for him to dispute. With each new witness, his heart beat faster, wondering if the district attorney would call Jennie to present her version. But the day ended and she had neither appeared nor been called to the witness stand.

Returning home that evening, Newt felt more drained and tired than ever before in his life. It was like he'd been fed through his own production machines, cut and folded until he formed a box that could hold all the different stories of what happened that night.

◆

The second day of the trial dawned with bitter cold. The sunlight seemed pale and weak as it rose through the icy fog. Newt looked out of his bedroom window through a thick layer of frost. He felt exhausted still, even after sleeping the sleep of the dead for nearly ten hours. He struggled to gather himself and dress for the day. He could hear the teakettle whistling in the kitchen as he made his way downstairs.

George was at the dining room table eating bacon and eggs. "Good morning. I thought you'd never rise. Sit down, you still have time for breakfast."

"No, thanks," Newt said. "But I could use a cup of tea."

"You look like you could use a bit more than that, man. How much weight have you lost? Your clothes hang on you like a scarecrow's."

Newt sighed and pulled out a chair. The housekeeper brought him a plate of food and a cup of hot tea, and he picked at his eggs absentmindedly while George recounted the testimony of the day before.

"No need to worry about the witness testimony yesterday. I spoke with Judge Sutton, and he's confident the district attorney is making a tactical error. By focusing on the events that occurred afterward, he's failing to establish intent."

Newt nodded and continued to poke at his food.

"Just wait until your team starts to present their defense. Judge Sutton assures me that Mr. Watson is among the finest orators in the state. His arguments will be something worth watching."

When they left for court it was painfully cold outside. The wind stung his cheeks and made Newt wish for a scarf. As they approached the courthouse, they could see the crowd already gathered on the steps. Even in this frigid weather, there was a line of people stretching out across the lawn; mostly men and boys, but a few women as well, bundled against the cold and pressing close to the front doors, banging to be let in. Newt and George slipped unnoticed around the back of the building and entered through the clerk's office.

Sutton and Watson were already at the table as they entered. They greeted them with firm handshakes and assurances that things were going well.

At nine a.m., the outside door was opened and the crowd came surging into the room, men climbing over the backs of the benches to secure good seats. Within minutes the hall was full and the constable was turning people away from the door.

Judge Haight entered the chamber at half past nine, nodding to the attorneys and commenting that he was glad to see that the court clerk, Pease, hadn't frozen to death in the night.

Newt listened as the district attorney called upon the coroner, then Dr. Morse again. Perhaps George was right, that it was a mistake on the district attorney's part to focus on what happened after the murder, or perhaps he was just trying to keep up his spirits. As the day wore on, Newt's mood and demeanor darkened.

The testimony continued as the innkeeper of the National Hotel and his wife were called upon to testify about Newt's suspicious and peculiar behavior in the days leading up to the events. They painted a picture of a confused, incoherent man not fully in control of his senses, and it hurt to think back on those days and recall the fervor, the madness that consumed him. Upon cross-examination, Watson probed deeper into the innkeepers' perception of Newt's behavior. It seemed as if he was encouraging them to call Newt mad.

Perhaps he had been a madman, as his defense attorneys would set out to convince the jury, but Newt could hardly see where that was helping his cause.

Finally, after lunchtime, Palmer was called to testify. He went to the stand in his finest clothes, turning to smile at Newt as he passed. He didn't seem the least bit worried. Taking the oath and sitting down, he responded to the district attorney's questions deliberately and with clear enunciation.

"Mr. Palmer, can you recount for us how you came to learn of the infidelity of Mr. Rowell's wife?"

"Certainly. Around the middle of last year, some mail was mistakenly delivered to the office that was intended for Mrs. Rowell. Upon receiving it, I opened it and discovered a correspondence from the deceased, making statements that were of an improper tone for addressing a married woman. Upon reading the letter, I sealed it up and had it taken to Mrs. Rowell at once. Within a day she came to the office to accuse me of spying on her."

"Did Mr. Rowell say anything with regards to the letter?" North asked.

"I asked Mr. Rowell if his wife said anything to him about my opening her private letter. He said she had, and that she complained to him that I had tampered with her mail. About that time, Mr. Rowell changed his manner toward me, and his relations became rather cool and distant. I asked Rowell again the same question, if his wife had complained that I opened some of her letters, and pursued the subject. Rowell said she had, and that she had shown him the back of an envelope that had been opened before it reached her door. I asked him why she didn't show him the contents of the letter as well, and he said he didn't know, but she didn't do it. I said, 'I know very well why she will not show you the contents. Every time you go away on a trip of any duration, she has a letter similar to the one of which she showed you a part, and in my opinion they come from Johnson Lynch.' Rowell hastily inquired, 'What?! Is she carrying on a correspondence with that man? I didn't know she was corresponding with him!'"

These comments stabbed Newt like a knife. It wasn't that Palmer was recounting the facts for the court, but that he seemed to be enjoying it. He was embellishing every detail to paint Newt as a fool.

"What happened then, after you informed Mr. Rowell?"

"I told him I believed that she left town to meet Lynch in Rochester on the second of August. I told Rowell that she had been away prior to that, and I could give him facts showing that she had had an improper relationship with Lynch. Mr. Rowell, as I remember, made no reply, and I do not recall anything further being said that day."

"Was that the end of the matter?" asked North.

"No. Subsequently, I told Rowell that I once had a conversation with his wife and she complained about his lack of affection. She used the expression 'He's as cold as an iceberg' and added that she felt justified in having other company."

A murmur ran through the crowd. Newt couldn't believe what he was hearing. Smiling broadly, Palmer continued.

"I told her she was not justified, but merely had an excuse. I told Rowell that I heard her say that he was very slow in finding out things about her, and that she could do many things that would escape his observation. I told Rowell that she also said while she lived in Utica that she was going to have a tall boy with a straight nose, and that nobody at 97 Howard Avenue would be the father of it. I told Rowell at another time she had admitted to me that she had been with Johnson Lynch a year and a half previous."

After two days of monotonous facts and details of the murder scene, these colorful revelations caused a stir of excitement in the room. Newt felt humiliated. Finally, Judge Haight interrupted the testimony to admonish the crowd and return the court to order.

Palmer continued. "Rowell used to be away from two days to four weeks, two or three times a year. I told him that in July last, when he was away, she received a letter from Lynch, and that two days later I watched her on the way to the station. Late the same night, after a train from Rochester arrived, I saw her go to the family house. I marked that date on my calendar and told Rowell he had better make a search for himself, in case I was mistaken. I asked him later if he found out anything, and he replied, 'I have found enough.'"

Palmer smiled, clearly basking in the attention. He would have gone on all night had District Attorney North not cut him off and thanked him for his testimony before asking the judge to adjourn for the evening.

While the newspapers had already made a sensation of the case, Palmer's testimony represented a goldmine. The reporters scribbled furiously in their notebooks to catch every word before hurrying out of the courthouse to submit their stories for the morning papers.

The raised eyebrows of Sutton and Watson told Newt all he needed to know about his outlook. Clearly they had not expected any sort of information like Palmer had presented. They excused themselves to a quick supper at the hotel; they had a long night ahead of them discussing strategy for the morning.

Leaving the courthouse through the now customary crush of well-wishers, Newt's spirits reached their lowest point. He walked home silently next to George, contemplating spending his remaining days among murderers in the state prison. Surely after Palmer's betrayal the jury would send him to the gallows.

♦

Batavia's Murder Trial
CLOSE OF THE CASE FOR THE PROSECUTION

William T. Palmer continues his story of what led to the killing of Johnson L. Lynch.

Batavia, N.Y., Jan 25 - There was manifestly an increased interest in the trial of E. Newton Rowell today for the killing of Johnson L. Lynch, of Utica. The testimony that Rowell's partner, William T. Palmer, gave yesterday afternoon stimulated the curiosity of the public so that everybody, it seemed, had the greatest desire to hear him continue his story of how he laid the foundation for the horrible tragedy of the 30th of October. The excited crowd stood in the frosty air in front of the locked door a long time before it was opened, evidently in forgetfulness of the fact that the atmosphere was so frigid that the mercury in the village thermometer indicated 6 below zero. The Judge, counsel and prisoner were prompt in attendance, and when as many of the multitude had been admitted as the court room could accommodate, the venerable crier mumbled over the form that opened the court, the jurors answered to their names, and Mr. Palmer resumed his seat in the witness box. He seems to be pleased with the unenviable notoriety his questionable relations with the case has given him, and he speaks slowly, in order, he says, laughingly, that the score of reporters will have no difficulty in following him. He took up his narrative where he left off when court adjourned last night. - N.Y. Times, Jan.25, 1884

"I told Rowell on several occasions," Palmer began, "that he had right and justice on his side and that he would have my support and assistance in anything he would do in the matter in strict accordance with the law, and that his wife could not make out a case against him, and, said I, if you confine yourself to strictly legal methods you will have public sympathy on your side, and you don't want to do anything that will turn any portion of it to

133

the other side."

"Did you suggest to the defendant at any time that he should go away on a business trip?" the district attorney asked.

"I think I at first suggested it to him, and that I should watch the mails and if anything came addressed to her in a certain, peculiar hand, as I always considered Lynch's, that I could inform him. I told Rowell that Lynch would probably come to his house if he had an opportunity, and that Rowell could come home and secret himself in the cellar and hear what was said in the room over his head, and that before he should go away he should fix two or three windows so that he could get in readily."

"And what did Mr. Rowell say in response?" asked North.

"Rowell said I could watch in the house, but I told him that I had rather not, that all I could do was assist him. I told Rowell that if Lynch discovered him he might crush him, or throw him out the window without taking pains to open it."

Laughter once again broke out in the courtroom. Each new comment was another wound in Newt's side.

Palmer continued, "I told Rowell he ought to provide himself with a club, or some weapon, and perhaps some pepper. Lynch would be a hard man to handle, but if Mr. Rowell could throw pepper in his eyes he would be at his mercy. Rowell said if he should go up there and discover a gentleman making a friendly call he wouldn't want to make a disturbance. I told Rowell to get a pair of rubbers that he could put on over his stockings and they would enable him to walk about the house noiselessly."

"Did at any point you suggest to Mr. Rowell that you would assist him in these endeavors?"

"Yes, and furthermore, I told Rowell that I engaged two young men to assist us in our plan. Rowell said he would like to mark Lynch, so that Mrs. Rowell would no longer see any beauty in him, and I told him that if he resorted to any violence or injury to Lynch it would turn public sympathy to a great extent against him, and that it was unnecessary. I also told him that we could, if we found him in an improper condition in the house, turn him out in that condition, and being a proud and sensitive man, he would feel it much more than any physical punishment. I told Rowell that when he gave us admittance, somebody could rush in suddenly, and if these parties were in bed, we could seize Lynch's clothes and send them to him by express."

"What did Mr. Rowell say to this proposition?" asked the district attorney.

Palmer answered, "Mr. Rowell said that it would be a good joke to send the different articles to different places, and that the money and jewelry could be sent to his mother, and his pantaloons, coat, vest, and shoes could be sent to the different Utica newspapers. I told Rowell that an account of the performance at his house would be published in Batavia, and that we could send a copy of the paper in each package. Mr. Rowell said he would leave home early in the morning. I had told Rowell that there was a hotel opposite the station, separated from it by a board fence, and that as it was a quiet place, he could station himself there and watch the trains. I advised him to put up at that hotel and go over to the station a few minutes before the arrival of convenient trains from the east upon which Lynch might arrive from Utica, and if he should see his wife in the sitting room it would be a pretty good indication that Lynch was coming."

"Is that how Mr. Rowell came to learn when Mr. Lynch was arriving by train?" asked North.

"No," Palmer answered. "Mr. Rowell said he would leave me the key to his private box at the post office, and I think I suggested that I would go there just after the distribution of the evening mail and bring him any letters that I found addressed to his wife. That was how we learned which train he would be arriving on."

"Is there anything more that you discussed with Mr. Rowell?"

"During our conversation, there had been something said between Rowell and me about the children. The first time Rowell spoke of his children was shortly after I gave him the information concerning his wife, about the first of September. Mr. Rowell said, 'These children; I don't know what I shall do with them. If I thought it would punish her more to have to work hard to support them than it would if I kept them, I would let her have them. But she could support herself easily without them and have a good time, and it would put me to considerable trouble and expense to take proper care of them.'"

Watson spoke up. "Your Honor, I object. These statements have no bearing upon Lynch's arrival from Utica."

Newt sat fixed in his chair, unable to cry out, unable to call Palmer the traitor he was and defend his own honor. Just then, several people in the audience began to shout their displeasure at Palmer. It was a shock to Newt, and he strained to see who had risen to his defense. Upon restoring order, Judge Haight threatened to remove to jail anyone who further disturbed the proceedings. The objection was sustained.

District Attorney North spoke up. "Mr. Palmer, could you please stay to the topic of what you and Mr. Rowell discussed when he was in residence at the National Hotel?"

Palmer continued. "At the hotel on Monday afternoon, Rowell said it was very tiresome there and requested me to bring him something lively to read. The next day, in the afternoon, I was at the hotel again, and I told him we had a piece of good luck. A telegram had just been delivered to the box factory addressed to Miss Jennie Rowell. It was opened and when I receipted for it I read it, sealed it, and sent it to Mrs. Rowell. It was dated Syracuse, and read like this: 'Will be up at seven,' and it was signed Jennie Lowery. I told him 'I don't believe she has got the telegram yet, but you have got the information.' I said I would speak to the boys. Rowell said in a meditative way, 'Jennie Lowery,' and he seemed surprised. I said to Rowell, 'He'll be around on the 6:30 train.'"

The district attorney asked, "Did you have any

further discussions with Mr. Rowell after that?"

Palmer replied, "I did not see Rowell again until after the shooting. When our party was on the way to his house, we met Rowell in the custody of the officers. Recognizing him, I stopped and said, 'Why, what are you doing here?' Mr. Rowell said, 'I am under arrest.' 'What for?' I asked him. He said, 'I have shot Lynch.' I think I inquired if he had hurt him seriously, and Rowell replied, 'He is dead.' Nothing further was said. I went to the justice's office where he was taken, and the next morning visited him in jail. We sat down on a bench and Rowell inquired of me where the man was hit, and I understood he was shot through the lungs. Rowell said, 'He was shot twice, then.' 'No,' I stated to him, 'there was only one wound, and that was through the body.' 'Why,' he said, 'I thought he must have been hit in the head.' I replied that he was not. Rowell told me that he found Lynch in the bedroom and that he had tried to put pepper in his eyes, but that he was such a big fellow he couldn't reach around him. 'He got up and came for me,' Rowell said, 'and I was afraid he would get hold of me, and I commenced shooting. He started and ran down the stairs, and I shot at him as fast as I could until I had emptied the pistol. I didn't know I had hit him with a bullet.'"

"Did Mr. Rowell identify Mr. Lynch as being the man that he had shot?" North asked.

"No," replied Palmer. "Mr. Rowell said it was dark, and he couldn't have told who it was."

At noon, the defense attorney, Mr. Watson, began the cross-examination. Palmer told his long story again as Watson probed for new evidence.

"Mr. Palmer, on what date did it come to your knowledge that Mrs. Rowell had accused you of surreptitiously opening her mail?" he asked.

"I cannot recall for certain, but it would have been around about July thirty-first last year."

"And how did you learn of this?"

"Mrs. Rowell came to the box factory one day while Mr. Rowell was out of town, in a fit of anger, and told me, 'It would be a little more agreeable to read my own letters first.'"

"Did Mrs. Rowell make this comment to you in confidence?"

"No, she made the remark in a loud tone and in the hearing of the employees of the factory."

"Did this accusation by Mrs. Rowell upset you?" asked Watson.

"Yes."

"Afterwards, in talking with Mr. Rowell on the subject of his wife's infidelity, was he open to what you had to say?" Watson asked.

"No, he was not," Palmer replied.

"Did you continue to bring up the topic with Mr. Rowell in the days that followed?"

"Yes, sir."

"Did Mr. Rowell seem averse to making it the topic of conversation?"

"Yes, he said on one occasion that he did not think his wife would do such a thing, and wished to stop talking about it."

"And did you stop talking about it?"

"No, sir, I felt it my duty as a friend to reveal the

truth."

"Mr. Palmer, did Mr. Rowell exhibit any strange behavior around the office once he had been told about his wife's actions?"

"Yes, he would sit at his table and bury his face in his hands and be very absentminded. Sometimes he would talk aloud, addressing his conversation to no one in particular, and on one occasion I overheard him murmur, 'She was such a pretty woman.'"

"Mr. Palmer, in your opinion, did Mr. Rowell usually speak of his children affectionately?"

"Yes, he was quite an affectionate father. He usually brought something to them when he returned from his business trips."

"Mr. Palmer, would you agree that once you had told Mr. Rowell of his wife's unfaithfulness, he became sad, dejected, and melancholy, and his appearance underwent a change?"

"Yes, I would agree with that statement."

Watson asked Palmer point by point who it was that developed and arranged what he called "the plot." Palmer answered every interrogation that he was the one who suggested everything, and that it was understood between him and Newt that his suggestions were to be adopted. Palmer stated that Newt did contemplate a business trip when he left home the Monday before the tragedy. It was distinctly understood, Palmer said, that no violence or brutality should be inflicted upon Lynch, and that he had suggested that Newt carry weapons, to be used only in the case of self-defense.

When Palmer was questioned further about

Newt's manner, he said he'd noticed a peculiar expression in Newt's eyes before the tragedy.

"Can you describe that expression?" asked Watson.

"It was an expression of complete despair—the perfect extinguishment of hope."

"Mr. Palmer, thank you for your frankness," Watson said. "I have one final question for you, and I would like to ask you to answer it with the utmost sincerity and honesty, and remind you of your oath before the court. In regard to your own relations with Mrs. Rowell, have you ever been intimate with her?"

The silence in the courtroom was absolute.

Palmer said, "Yes, on one occasion I embraced and kissed her, but I never committed any crime."

The crowd gasped, and Newt realized that his betrayal was complete.

♦

Jennie sat by the window of the room she was renting at Washburn House as the last of the daylight faded. Spread before her on the nightstand were copies of the local newspapers.

"Dear, you can't stay hidden in this room forever. Won't you please come downstairs and have a little supper?" her mother asked.

Jennie shook her head.

"Very well. I'll ask the hostess to bring a little something up to the room."

When her mother left the room, Jennie reached out and picked up the papers and began to read them again. She had read them so many times already she had lost count. Each time she hoped to find some new piece of information. Surely the court was adjourning for the day by now, and she would have to wait until the morning paper to learn what had happened.

The reporters had been relentless in trying to get a statement from her. Each time she refused. Finally, someone fabricated an interview and ran it in the morning paper, to great interest and sales. When she read it, she was furious, and sent a note to the reporter of the *Daily News* to come to her room so she could make a statement. Now she would have to wait until the next morning for the story to be set straight.

The trial was only a few days old and had adjourned for the weekend. The thought of another two days of waiting was agonizing. She had been called to town by a subpoena from the district attorney under the rationale that she might be called to testify, but two days into the trial, he had yet to summon her. So she spent her days at Washburn House watching the clock, waiting to be called upon, reading the previous day's testimony each morning and watching as her reputation was dismantled piece by piece. While she dreaded the humiliation of having to stand in front of a room full of strangers, she was looking forward to standing defiant in front of them all. She had suffered enough already. Her children were taken from her, her home destroyed, the one man she truly loved was dead. Now to sit idly by and watch pious hypocrites relish each sordid detail of her life was more than she could bear.

CHAPTER TWENTY-TWO

The trial resumed on Monday morning as, one by one, Judge Sutton called Newt's family, friends, and acquaintances to the stand. He questioned them all about Newt's disposition, and especially his propensity to nervousness and anxiety. Sitting and watching his friends and family as they answered questions and recounted stories about his infirmities and his mind, Newt felt as if his character was being burned down to the wick, until finally his shame guttered and went out. He placed his head down on the table. For the rest of the afternoon, he contemplated whether the hangman's noose or a life in a cage would be the better fate.

Even the crowd seemed to have lost interest, and the days dragged slowly by. Finally, on the afternoon of the thirtieth, the defense closed its case. Newt walked home with his brother, wondering if it would be one of his last days of freedom.

"Just wait until tomorrow, Newt. Have faith. Mr. Watson and Judge Sutton will not let you down. Tomorrow you will see the results of the case they've been building all week. After tomorrow, there is not a jury in the world that would hesitate to set you free."

Newt did not sleep well that night. He had begun to doubt his own memories, and could not be sure which were his and which were the words of others. Is truth really that slippery, he wondered, that it can shift and change depending upon one's perspective? Is trying to capture truth like trying to keep a river in a box? Is man just another vessel incapable of containing all that it encounters?

◆

At four o'clock on the afternoon of January thirtieth, the defense began its closing arguments. Mr. Watson rose and stepped before the jury.

"Gentlemen of the jury, three months ago to the day, this community was startled by the report that an adulterer had entered the house of one of the most worthy and respected citizens of Batavia, debauched his wife, disgraced his children, blasted his life and ruined his home, and the worthy citizen entered the house and killed the adulterer. In his madness at discovering the beautiful wife he so deeply loved in the very act of adultery, he shot the man. These were the circumstances under which the tragedy was committed.

"Everywhere, by the voice of the press, the story was told. In this country, an American citizen under all circumstances and in all cases believes in protecting the purity of his home and his domestic relations. Never before has a jury been selected with greater care than in this case. It was an extraordinary case." He swept his arms towards the packed gallery. "Crowds thronged about the temple of justice. Tables were crowded with reporters. Is it," Watson said, turning back towards the jury, "because the people are afraid that some great criminal is to be let loose on them? No! It is because everywhere the sentiment is that E. Newton Rowell is an innocent man. It is a part of the instincts of humanity. The wronged and injured husband should not have additional suffering and sorrow put upon him unless the law of the land absolutely requires it. In a few hours, this community will be electrified by the verdict you will bring in. It will bring joy or sorrow to the hearts of the virtuous men and women of this country."

Newt listened to Watson implore the jury and was amazed by his hyperbole. Watson spoke with the enthusiasm of a revivalist preacher, pacing back and forth between the defense table and the jury rail. Watson claimed to be speaking in the interest of justice and morality, for "pure wives, pure homes, and pure domestic relations." The eyes of the jury were fixed on him as if he were an Old Testament prophet come down to earth. Clearly, George had not exaggerated the man's abilities when he called him among the finest orators in the state.

"This jury," Watson continued, "is to decide

whether a man may invade another man's home with impunity—whether the adulterer is to be protected, or justice is to be done."

Turning again, Watson pointed toward Newt. "Mr. Rowell is glad to be here and is willing to trust his fate to you. If you should decide that for doing his duty he is to spend his time behind bars among burglars, thieves—common felons—to your judgment he will submit.

"The senior counsel for the prosecution, in saying that the children were brought in court to be put up as a shield between the prisoner and justice, was unjust and unmerited. They have been in the charge of their aunt, who was obliged to be in court. She had no alternative but to bring them with her.

"I am not here to appeal to the sympathies of the jury, but to ask you to remember the claims of society and of these children, and save them from the sorrow which would fall upon them if their father was convicted of a crime of which he was not guilty. A juror without sympathy has no intelligence, no heart, no humanity. He is only part of a competent juror.

"You have seen the prisoner here," said Watson, gesturing to Newt again, "passive, the least excited of anyone in the room, and caring the least, apparently, about the result; a man upon whose face you can see the shadow of the sorrow and disgrace that fell upon him when Johnson L. Lynch, the vile adulterer, seduced his wife from the path of rectitude. We need not go very far outside the legal facts to demonstrate that Johnson L. Lynch was unworthy the decent regard of any respectable citizen, unmarried, an outcast who sought to pull down and disintegrate society, travelling one hundred and sixty miles to break into the house of an honest citizen to practice his hellish arts, with five dollars in his pocket and a diamond stud in his necktie.

"Furthermore, there is not a particle of evidence in the case showing Jennie Rowell had been guilty of any other impropriety than being led to forget her marriage vows and her duty to her husband and her children through the arts and machinations of Johnson L. Lynch. This is all that can be said against her. One would have supposed that the children's presence and prattle in the house would have restrained Mrs. Rowell. There is no evidence that Mrs. Rowell had relations with Lynch until she moved to Batavia. If she did, there is no evidence that Rowell knew anything about it, except some fragmentary statements not worth remembering. It is shown that they had been happy in their family relations. The defendant's love, affection, and devotion to his wife and children were something almost sublime. If nothing else demonstrates his love, consider the fact that in his limited circumstances he tried to build and pay for a beautiful home for them in our village. There is nothing to show that he had any reason to suspect his wife's fidelity until Palmer told him. For reasons known in part and part unknown, and that must be left to speculation to determine, Palmer learns or becomes advised of Mrs. Rowell's frailty. She charged him with opening her letters, and this made him angry. Maybe before he had not felt it his duty to tell Rowell, but he determined to do so when she upbraided him. Never mind what his motives were.

"Gentlemen, I admire the zeal of the district attorney, but regret that it was not in a better cause than punishing a husband for killing an adulterer in his own home. Something that three fourths of the men of family in this community would do, just as Rowell did, under the same circumstances. When hope is dead, men will submit to the inevitable. When Rowell got in that condition where common-sense people say that he was practically insane—when, to use the language of Palmer, 'there was in his face a look of blank despair—the utter extinguishment of hope'—he was mere clay in the hands of the potter. He had lost his individuality. The potter had no more trouble to mould and wield the clay than Palmer did to sway Rowell in the vacillating and diseased condition of his mind. He completely surrendered himself to this devious friend."

The comments made Newt's face flush with embarrassment and shame. To be betrayed by Palmer was one thing, but to have that betrayal broadcast in the courtroom was an entirely new level of humiliation.

"There has been a good deal of talk about a plan to entrap and entice Lynch; also about premeditation, deliberation, and intent. Where is it except in the conduct of Palmer, who laid plans, concocted schemes, attended to the details? If a man suspects his wife's fidelity, there is no law, moral or otherwise, to prevent him from watching her; and if, while he was so engaged, some act of adultery was committed within his view, and he shot the adulterer, some prosecuting attorney is to stand up and howl about his intentions? It is the duty of a man to place his wife under surveillance if he has reason to suspect her. Palmer's statement about what Rowell said relative to the punishment of his wife by abandoning his children to her, if he caught her in adultery, was dragged into the case by the prosecution to cast reproach on a kind husband and an affectionate father who was devoted to those children, and thus create prejudice in the minds of the jury. You see in the nature of things that Palmer's plans, thoughts, ideas are put into the mouth of Rowell. Whatever you want to do with him, don't imagine that Edward Newton Rowell will ever surrender those little children to his faithless wife.

"Everybody hopes against a certainty until it overtakes them. There Rowell was in that hotel without weapons. What he did there shows his vacillation and instability. Palmer urged him to stay, and succeeded in keeping him there. Several curious and strange pieces of good luck came to Palmer that Tuesday, among which was the delivery of an unsealed telegram at his office. The signature was that of a woman, and Rowell's meditative reflection upon the name of Jennie Lowery shows that he was in doubt. It was a suspicious circumstance, and the pendulum swung to Palmer's side of the story. Mr. Rowell was undoubtedly so distressed that he did not know what he was doing. Talk about insanity! What greater insane act than pulling out the picture of his wife in a dark hall and saying to the hotel proprietor,

'I am after the man that is after that woman?' What more insane act than to register a fictitious name and then tell the innkeeper his right name, residence and business? What sense is there in such conduct? Palmer stuck to Rowell all day and kept talking to him. Everything Rowell did when in his presence proved he was a man suffering from mental disturbance."

Watson stood facing the jury, his arms outstretched and palms upraised. He looked into the eyes of each one of the jurors before turning to face the bench. Then, lowering his head, he said, "Your Honor, it is at this point that I would request to adjourn for the day and finish my comments in the morning."

When the case was suspended for the night, the excitement and buzz through the crowd was electric. The crowd dispersed into the street and into the taverns, spreading the news in a manner that only magnified the drama, each one of them secure in their authority of having witnessed the great trial in person.

Newt returned home, wondering again if it would be his last night spent in freedom. It was a cheerless and tense evening as they gathered around the supper table. George and Julia did their best to distract him with the mundane events of the day, but Newt's thoughts never strayed from the doubts about where his future lay.

The next day began with the conclusion of Watson's statements. He continued for another two and a half hours with as much fervor as he had displayed the previous afternoon. There was no mistake that the jury was in his thrall. His defense hinged upon three different points, all of which he advocated passionately. They were justification, self-defense, and insanity. To Newt's dismay he paid the greatest attention to the theory of insanity, recounting for the jury the testimony of Newt's family and friends that clearly showed the fragility of his mental state and the uncharacteristic behavior which he exhibited in the days leading up to the tragedy. He reminded them of the great physical disparity between Lynch and Rowell and pointed out that no one had offered any evidence that Rowell had not acted out of self-defense. Then he spoke bitterly of Lynch, denouncing him as a professional, degraded libertine and adulterer who made it a business of seducing married women, and laid the blame of the situation carefully at the feet of Palmer, who he insisted had orchestrated the entire event.

Following a short break for dinner, District Attorney North took the floor for the prosecution and recounted the evidence against Newt, recalling for the jury in detail the innkeeper's testimony about Newt's behavior at the National Hotel. He spoke of how Newt had obtained a gun and pepper for the express purpose of attacking the victim. He spoke of how Lynch was in the house for over an hour before Newt chose to act.

"Are these the actions of a man overcome with emotion? Or are they the measured actions of a man in control of his senses, who knew exactly what he wanted to do when he entered that bedroom? Gentlemen, I do not dispute the good character of this man seated before you. I have no doubt that he is a capable and loving father. I merely present to you the facts of the case as you have heard them from the mouths of the people who witnessed them. The actions of Mr. Rowell on the night of October thirtieth were not the ravings of a madman overcome with emotion, but the carefully planned and executed machinations of a man bent on revenge."

He continued to recount the evidence, and took care to recall the exactness of the law and exhort the jury to put aside emotion and decide the case based on the facts before them.

When he was finished, Judge Haight gave instructions to the jury. As Newt listened, he was impressed by the judge's eloquent and impartial manner. After two days of dramatic and emotional appeals from the attorneys, it was reassuring to hear a clear and rational recounting. Like an accountant checking his books, Judge Haight instructed the jury in the finer points of the charge of manslaughter and explained how they should consider the evidence. At 5:25 p.m., the case was handed to the jury, and recess was ordered until seven o'clock. The jury filed out of the courtroom and was taken across the street to the St. James Hotel, where it had been quartered since the opening of the trial.

Newt was to remain in custody until the verdict was reached, so he accompanied Sheriff Southworth to his home beside the jail. It provided some comfort to be in the presence of Southworth and his family. They ate and carried on as if it were any other day, which was easier than the unbearable tension of

Newt's own family. So relaxed was the supper that Southworth lost track of the time, and by the time they returned to the courthouse it was twenty past seven. To their surprise, the jury had already returned and was awaiting their appearance.

The courtroom was packed as usual with an anxious crowd barely able to contain its excitement. After apologizing to the judge and the court, Newt took his seat alongside Sutton and Watson and waited to hear the verdict.

The clerk rose and addressed the foreman of the jury. "Gentlemen of the jury, have you agreed upon a verdict?"

"We have."

"Do you find the prisoner guilty or not guilty?"

"Not guilty."

The hall resonated with cheers and applause.

"Upon what ground do you place the verdict?" asked the clerk.

"Upon the ground of self-defense," answered the foreman.

When the foreman uttered the words "Not guilty," Newt dropped his head into his hands and tears of joy poured from his eyes. Watson and Sutton were the first to clap him on the back and congratulate him, and he soon regained his composure. The court promptly discharged Newt from custody and in an instant he was surrounded by sympathizers who poured congratulations down upon him. George and his parents pushed their way through the throng, and he embraced them as their eyes welled with tears.

Hands were thrust out in front of him, grabbing

his own and shaking it vigorously. Faces moved before him, some he recognized, others total strangers.

He heard a familiar voice calling out from behind him, "Newt! Newt! Congratulations!"

Turning, he saw Palmer push through the crowd towards Newt with his hand extended. "Newt! I am so glad of the verdict. I knew all along you'd be found innocent."

Newt looked at him coolly and turned toward another person calling his name, and Palmer was lost in the crowd again.

Slowly the courtroom began to empty. George placed his coat over his shoulders and said, "C'mon Newt, I think we've spent enough time in this courtroom for one lifetime."

They made their way outside as the officers worked to clear the stragglers from the room. Crossing the street to the Washburn House, they were followed by the enthusiastic crowd that had gathered outside as news of the verdict had spread through the town. Newt was swept through the doors of the inn on the waves of a crowd cheering "Three cheers for Rowell!"

Blushing with embarrassment, he made for the stairs and George led him up to the room at the top of the landing where Julia and the girls were waiting for him. With tears in his eyes, he embraced them. One by one, Newt greeted his family, his legal team, and the business associates that had gathered there.

The crowd at the bottom of the stairs began to chant his name.

George placed a hand on his shoulder. "Newt, I think you'd better step out onto the landing and say a few words before they start to tear the place down."

Laughing, Newt handed Clara to George and stepped outside to a great roar of cheers. He descended to the lower steps and held his hands up for quiet.

"Gentlemen, I am glad to see you."

A roar went up from the crowd.

"Thank you. Thank you all for coming to support me. No man could ever have asked for more."

The crowd of men and boys began to file past him at the bottom of the steps and Newt shook the hand of each and every one, looking them in the eye to offer his thanks. When he had thanked everyone, he stepped back up the stairs and said loudly, "Gentlemen, I must now say goodnight to you all."

"No! Join us for a drink!" someone shouted from the back.

Laughter ran through the room. When it quieted, Newt said, "Thank you, but I have some little girls upstairs who are waiting for me." The crowd cheered as he turned and climbed back up the stairs.

Outside in the street, the gathering throng numbered over five hundred people. Two large bonfires were lit to keep off the chill of the subzero weather. Bottles were being passed around and the flames glowed orange against the white walls of the courthouse. Looking out the window of his hotel room, Newt watched in amazement and began to wonder if they would ever leave. Roman candles were lit and fireworks were discharged, and the general mayhem resembled New Year's Eve. After two hours had passed and the crowd showed no sign of dispersing, he left the hotel through a rear window and descended a ladder the proprietor had provided. George followed him down, and together they hurried through the darkness towards home.

CHAPTER TWENTY-THREE

The April sun shone pale through a layer of gauzy clouds. The horse's hooves stuck in the mud of the road as Newt rode beneath the golden yellow buds blooming on the branches overhead. It had been years since he had rented a horse from a livery stable and gone riding in the countryside. After years of riding in hacks he had forgotten the freedom he felt when mounted. The fields along the roadside were still muddy brown, and the dried stalks of the last year's corn harvest protruded from their loamy furrows.

Much time had passed since the trial, and he had been preoccupied with the legal and financial matters of the divorce. The house had been sold, and he had taken an apartment on East Main Street. He had still not returned to work, but had set aside enough money from selling his share of the business back to Palmer that he was in no difficulty. His sister Julia was looking after the children in Utica. He'd spent most of the past few weeks there as the final arrangements were being made. Now all that was left was to sign the paper, and eight years of marriage would be undone.

As his horse crested the rise in the hillside, he could see the white frame of the farmhouse stark against the fertile valley. A thin column of wood smoke rose from the chimney, and in the garden was the stooped figure of a man hoeing the rows for planting.

He had hoped to find Jennie alone. He resigned himself to uncomfortable small talk with her parents. He bore them no ill will, but was certain the feeling was not mutual. Certainly they felt the shame of the scandal too, and having their daughter back home only made them the subject of more scrutiny. He was certain they would rather he accept her back and take her off their hands.

As he neared the house, he was startled to realize that the figure in the garden was not Jennie's father, but rather a slight woman wearing a large overcoat. The tumble of gold hair pinned up beneath a straw hat gave her away. It was Jennie.

She did not hear him approaching until he was nearly to the garden gate, when she looked up, startled to see him.

"Why, Mr. Rowell? What brings you here? Is there something wrong?"

"No, Jennie, it's nothing like that. The girls are

fine."

Dismounting, he led his horse to the hitching post as Jennie put down the hoe and brushed dirt from her hands. She crossed the garden to meet him.

"Then what brings you out here? When we met last week I was under the belief that things had been finalized."

"Yes, indeed, they have. I just have something I wanted to discuss."

Opening the gate, her overshoes caked with soft clumps of earth, she said, "You'll have to forgive my appearance. I wasn't expecting company. Come, let's go up to the house."

Following her to the porch steps, Newt hesitated. "There's no need to go inside. Please, let's just have a seat here."

Jennie turned as she reached the top step and eyed him suspiciously. The porch was empty of furniture at this point in the season, so she stepped back down and took a seat on the top step. Newt climbed up and sat down beside her.

Taking his hat into his hand, he said, "I needed to see you one more time, to be sure there was no other way."

Jennie let out a short and scornful laugh. "You would take me back? After all of this?" She shook her head. "You are a strange man, Newt. As long as I live, I will never understand what goes through your head."

Looking down and averting his eyes, Newt continued. "It's just that I've been thinking. Who gives a damn what others think, Jennie?" He paused and looked up at her again. "Some days I feel as if the whole world has burned down around me, and then I think, what does it matter? It is our life to live. If we should choose to . . ." His voice trailed off.

"Newt, you don't understand. I don't want to go back. I have had enough of being someone's property."

Her words stung, and he turned to look at her again. He could see the defiance in her eyes, smoldering right below the surface. Perhaps she was right. Maybe he would never understand her, or what she wanted.

"Newt, we have known it for years but refused to admit it. The life you want has always been different from the one that I dreamed of."

He nodded his head, "What is it you want, Jennie?"

She looked off into the distance. "My freedom. Marriage feels like a prison to me now." A lone hawk circled over the hillside, high on a current of air. "I want to live on my own terms, and not those of another."

She paused, and as she turned back to him, he could see tears forming around the edges of her eyes. "I've decided to go west, find work, and live on my own. In a place like Chicago it doesn't matter who you are or where you came from."

He thought of the city, wrapped in smoke, its streets teeming with people, and tried to imagine her there.

"That is the life that I have always wanted, Newt. Not the one that you aspired to."

They sat in silence for a long moment before she spoke again.

"What will become of you, Newt?"

Newt hesitated for a moment, then said, "I will return to Batavia. I've talked with several bankers who have agreed to back me in starting my own company. It's strange, but I seem to have more friends there now than I did before."

"What will you do?" she asked.

Smiling a wry smile, he laughed and said, "Drive Palmer out of business."

Jennie smiled and let out a short laugh. "Well, that is one venture that I wish you much success with."

"I suppose this is goodbye, then."

"Yes, I suppose it is."

Taking her hand up to his mouth, he kissed it and said, "Goodbye, Jennie."

"Goodbye, Mr. Rowell. I hope someday you find the happiness that has eluded you."

He walked back to his horse and mounted it, then tipped his cap to her. She smiled and raised her hand to wave goodbye as if he were going off to work.

Newt brought the horse up to a trot and set off down the road. His cheeks were flush, and his heart burned inside his chest. He knew this was truly the end. As he reached the top of the hill, he looked back toward the porch one more time. She was still sitting upon the top step watching him leave. The horse rocked with the steady rhythm of an engine as he lifted his arm and waved one last time.

She stood up with one hand over her eyes, and with the other she waved back. The sun glimmered on the windows, and in a moment, she was gone.

ABOUT THE AUTHOR

Thomas Gahr was born in Batavia, New York, and grew up around the corner from the Rowell Mansion. A lifelong interest in the stories and history of his hometown led him to research and write this novel about the circumstances surrounding the murder. This is his first book. He currently resides in Minneapolis, Minnesota with his wife and two children.